Ba

BLOOD

ANNE SCHRAFF

SADDLEBACK
PUBLISHING

URBAN UNDERGROUND

Bad Blood
Dark Secrets
Dark Suspicions
Deliverance
Guilt Trip
Hurting Time
I'll Be There
Leap of Faith
The Lost
Misjudged

No Fear
The Stranger
Time of Courage
To Catch a Dream
To Die For
Unbroken
The Unforgiven
Vengeance
The Water's Edge
Winners and Losers

SADDLEBACK
P U B L I S H I N G
www.sdlback.com

© **2014 by Saddleback Educational Publishing**

ISBN-13: 978-1-62250-766-5
ISBN-10: 1-62250-766-5
eBook: 978-1-61247-977-4

Printed in Guangzhou, China
NOR/1213/CA21302313

18 17 16 15 14   1 2 3 4 5

CHAPTER ONE

Ernesto Sandoval was planning to take his girlfriend, Naomi Martinez, to the movies tonight. He was ready for a great time like they usually had. Today, at Cesar Chavez High School where they were both seniors, Naomi seemed a little upset, but Ernesto was happy to have gotten an A in his AP History class, and he didn't pay much attention to Naomi.

He didn't think anything was seriously wrong. But the moment Naomi got into Ernesto's Volvo, her violet eyes were narrowed with unhappiness and her lower lip was quivering. "Ernie," she cried, "she is *really* coming to live with us! Mom's sister's kid, Carlotta, is coming for sure! Oh, Ernie!"

1

Ernesto did not know much about Naomi's cousin Carlotta Valencia, except that her aunt was having a hard time with her seventeen-year-old daughter. The Valencias lived out of town, some hundred or so miles north. Other than a few miserable visits during the year, Carlotta was not a major problem.

"So," Ernesto said as he drove, "what happened?"

"Carlotta and her mother had this terrible blowup, and Aunt Mia and Uncle Franco just lost it. They can't take her anymore. They've been threatening to send her down to our house, but the last fight did it. Aunt Mia begged Mom to let Carlotta move down here with us and finish her senior year at Chavez, and you know my mother. Naturally, Dad is totally against it, and I'm just sick about it. Dad goes, 'Like we need this little juvenile delinquent living with us,' but Mom begged and Dad gave in. It's only until June, until she graduates, but oh, Ernie …" Naomi groaned.

"Uh, I'm sorry, Naomi," Ernesto said. Naomi had mentioned Carlotta before, but not often. He knew she didn't like her cousin, but he was vague on the details.

"She's such a jerk, Ernie," Naomi said. "I've only been with her a few times when we went up there to visit or she came down. I was so happy when it was over. Aunt Mia and Uncle Franco have two other kids, nice little girls. I'd love to have Maggie and Ali here instead of her."

Naomi Martinez usually got along with everyone, and Ernesto was really surprised by the depth of her unhappiness.

"That bad, huh?" Ernesto said. He'd seen Carlotta Valencia only once when she had been visiting the Martinez house last summer. Ernesto remembered it was right after Naomi's father, Felix, bought his pit bull, Brutus. Naomi's mother, Linda, was already terrified of the dog. It was a bad time for the Martinez family anyway, and Carlotta had made matters worse.

Carlotta kept insulting Mr. Martinez

3

that he was a cruel monster by forcing his wife to put up with a vicious, dangerous dog like Brutus. Brutus was actually a meek, lovable creature, and in time Linda Martinez loved him as much as the rest of the family. But Carlotta was determined to drive a wedge between Uncle Felix and Aunt Linda.

Ernesto remembered one night vividly. Felix Martinez stepped outside and said to Ernesto, "You know, Ernie, maybe I could just sic Brutus on the kid. You think that'd be okay if I got him to like rip her jeans, something like that, Ernie? Just to get rid of her, you know? I can't take much more."

Ernesto had vigorously advised against that course of action. But recalling the bitter feelings between Felix Martinez and Carlotta, Ernesto could hardly believe the man would consent to her coming to their home.

"Dad's gonna put her in the back bedroom, Zack's old room," Naomi said. "It's the smallest bedroom, and the heater doesn't work good. It's kind of grungy. Mom pleaded with Dad to get a new mattress for the bed because it's kind of lumpy, but Dad said it was good enough for Carlotta. Dad told Mom if she didn't stop making 'stupid suggestions' like getting a new mattress, he'd make Carlotta sleep on the porch with Brutus."

"Oh, brother," Ernesto said. He was beginning to think this date with Naomi was not going to be as much fun as he hoped.

"Carlotta is so boy crazy," Naomi continued bitterly. "She flirts with every guy she comes into contact with. She's just so brazen too. She wears her jeans like she's been poured into them. She weighs about fifteen pounds more than me, and we're the same height, but she insists on wearing the same size I do. She just looks slutty. She'll be wanting to borrow all my nice things, but I won't let her."

Ernesto was shocked. He loved Naomi with all his heart, but she was sounding like a really nasty person tonight.

Naomi cheerfully lent her sweaters to her friends Carmen, Mona Lisa, Yvette, almost anybody. Naomi was a beautiful girl who was more compassionate than almost anybody Ernesto knew. She was so bighearted she was willing to remove a cherished sweater and give it to a girl on the street who seemed cold. Now she actually seemed selfish and spiteful.

"I'm going to put a special lock on my closet so she can't get in, *ever,*" Naomi said.

"That's, uh … a good idea," Ernesto said, driving slowly through the heavy traffic on their way to the multiscreen theater. "Head off trouble before … you know … it starts." Ernesto was a good driver in his old Volvo, and he was proud of the fact that he had never gotten a ticket or been in an accident. The dents in the Volvo's fenders were inflicted by the previous owner.

"It's not that Aunt Mia and Uncle Franco are poor, Ernie. No way, Uncle Franco makes more money than Dad. He's a financial advisor. And Aunt Mia has these phony house parties where she trots out all these useless beauty products. Silly women think they're there to drink coffee and eat dainty little cookies, and they end up being pressured to buy some sixty-dollar bottle of cream supposedly guaranteed to make a sixty-year-old woman look twenty in six weeks. Lotta has more clothes than me, and expensive ones too. The only reason she doesn't look good in her clothes is that she buys two sizes too small," Naomi said.

"Oh man," Ernesto thought to himself. "This is not looking good. Where is my sweet, cheerful babe?" He sighed, then said, "You know, Naomi, maybe it won't work out, and she'll go home early. A lot of parents and kids fight, and Carlotta might want to split."

"Oh no," Naomi said bitterly through clenched teeth. "We're stuck with her until June. For years, her parents have been holding us, especially Dad, over her head. One more misstep and she gets the ultimate punishment—living with the Martinez family. The parents have lost control of her. When she went off the road this last time, it was over. We're the Devil's Island on Bluebird Street, and she's been condemned. Lotta cheated on her tests at that ritzy private school she goes to, and when the principal caught her, she called her 'a crazy old crone' right to her face. That did it. She was expelled. Now the boom has been lowered, and we're trapped."

"I hope at least you guys are getting paid for having her," Ernesto said, searching for a parking place in the underground lot.

"Oh, generously, but it's not worth it. They said they'd write a check if we had to spend extra. The Valencias are so happy to be getting rid of her that money is no object," Naomi said.

"Well, that's good anyway," Ernesto sighed. The movie was a clever animated feature that appealed to teens and adults. It was supposed to be hilarious. Ernesto was praying that it was so funny Naomi would forget her cousin, at least for a little while.

As they walked toward the theater, Naomi said, "I bet you think I'm a horrible person, Ernie. You must think I've been hiding all these dark impulses beneath my phony exterior, and Lotta coming has exposed me for what I am."

Ernesto stopped walking, turned, and grasped Naomi's shoulders firmly. He kissed her on her full, sweet lips.

"Babe, I think you're wonderful. Don't you dare say anything against the girl I love. There's not a phony bone in your body. You obviously have a lot of history with this girl, and you dread her coming to your house and disrupting everything. It'd be different if she was staying for the weekend, but this is long term. I don't blame you for being upset. It would be like Clay Aguirre moving into our little house on Wren Street. I'd run away from home."

Clay Aguirre and Naomi once dated, but when he abused her, she became Ernesto's girlfriend. Ernesto could not think of anyone he would rather avoid than Clay Aguirre.

He was arrogant, cruel, inconsiderate, and heartless, at least in Ernesto's opinion.

Naomi smiled. "Thanks for being so understanding, Ernie. Like I didn't know you would be! You're the only human being in the world I can safely dump on. Mom would start bawling, and Dad would go off the wall. If he knew how I really felt, he'd want me to help him barricade the house and keep Carlotta out when she appears. Dad is so angry about this that he's ready to explode, and all he needs is to know I feel the same way. Poor Mom wants to help her sister out with the monster. Poor Mom, it'd break her heart if we refused Carlotta. I can't pile on Mom like that."

"When is she coming?" Ernesto asked as they bought popcorn in the lobby of the theater.

"This weekend, Saturday morning," Naomi said with a shudder. "Her parents are bringing her down. Aunt Mia said she packed ten suitcases for her. *Ten suitcases*!"

The movie was very entertaining, and

Naomi would have been laughing a lot under ordinary circumstances. But she didn't laugh very much. Ernesto felt really bad. Naomi's mind was elsewhere. Ernesto could foresee that the weeks ahead would not be as much fun as they had been in the past. But, desperately trying to put a good spin on the situation, Ernesto tried to convince himself that maybe Carlotta wouldn't be as bad as Naomi feared once she settled in. Maybe they'd even sort of become friends, or, Ernesto worried, did stuff like that only happen in sappy movies?

"Well," Felix Martinez said on Saturday morning, "they're on their way. The Valencias are about to bring happiness back to their own home and mess up our lives here on Bluebird Street by depositing the monster here."

"She's not a monster," Linda Martinez said softly. "She's just a mixed-up seventeen-year-old girl. She needs guidance. My sister and my brother-in-law have been too tolerant, letting her get away with things. Deep down, she's not a bad girl."

"Yeah, well, I'll give her guidance all right," Mr. Martinez said. "I'll guide her right out to the porch where she can sleep with Brutus the first time she causes trouble around here. If there's one thing I can't stand, it's a punk teenager."

Naomi sat at the computer, trying to complete a paper for English. It was no use. Her concentration was shot. How could she think about and analyze the convoluted poetry of T. S. Eliot for Ms. Lauer's class when disaster was about to strike her own home?

"There they are!" Mom cried out, almost screaming, and adding to the horror of the moment.

"Oh, for Pete's sake," Dad snarled.

Aunt Mia seemed to be dragging a sobbing Carlotta from the backseat of the car. A witness would probably immediately have called the police and reported a kidnapping underway. Uncle Franco was already unloading the first of the ten suitcases, which had grown to twelve. He staggered under the weight of the suitcases as he made his way up the Martinez driveway.

"Help him, Felix," Linda pleaded. "Please help him."

"Oh, for Pete's sake," Felix Martinez growled as he got out of his chair. He cast a dark look at the sobbing teenager who was now hanging desperately onto her seat belt to keep from being pulled from the car.

"Please, Mommy," Carlotta was screaming. "Don't make me stay here. Please let me come home, Mommy. I promise I'll be good. I'll go on my knees and apologize to Ms. Fenwick for calling her a crazy old crone. I'll get on my knees and kiss her hand!"

"Carlotta," Uncle Franco said in a weary voice. "Ms. Fenwick said if you ever set foot on the campus of that school again, she is going to call the police. Calling her an old crone was bad enough but you also spit in her face."

"I didn't, I didn't—" Carlotta wept, "that was an accident!"

Mia Valencia finally pried her daughter from the car, and Linda Martinez joined the pair.

"Lotta, sweetheart," Mrs. Martinez said, "we're all family. We care about you. Come on now and stop your crying and come in the house. I've made some nice hot chocolate, Mexican chocolate, all frothy and yummy, and I made some flan."

"I don't want any stupid Mexican chocolate or flan," Carlotta yelled. "I want to go home!"

At this moment Felix Martinez, who had been lugging suitcases into the house and was already feeling it in his back, stopped in front of the girl and said, "You ain't goin' home, Lotta. Deal with it. I don't want you here any more than you wanna be here. It's gonna be a pain you-know-where for everybody. Stop your slobbering and try to act like the adult you almost are," he yelled.

14

Carlotta looked at her Uncle Felix with pure hatred. She launched into another more hysterical round of sobs. When Linda Martinez put her arm around the girl's shoulders and attempted to lead her up the walk to the front door, Carlotta wrenched free and tried to leap into her mother's arms. She howled, "Mommmmmmeeeeee!"

Felix Martinez opened the front door, and his gaze met Naomi's. "Oh, this is beautiful. Ain't this beautiful?" he said. "Ain't this everybody's dream of a lovely Saturday morning? Kid, I'd rather be on the forklift!"

Carlotta's father took a grim grip of his daughter's arm. "Carlotta, you defied all the rules. You laughed at the curfews. We told you if one more outrage happened, you were coming here. You were warned. Now make the best of it. Carlotta, try to learn from this experience and become a better person," he said as he led his daughter toward the front door.

"I hate you, Daddy," Carlotta hissed.

The man shrugged. He'd heard those words before from his eldest daughter. It didn't break his heart anymore. It just made him more resolute than ever that something drastic had to be done.

"We'll call you every day, darling," Mia Valencia said. She reached for her daughter for a good-bye embrace, but Carlotta turned her back and stood like a frozen statue as her parents hurried away.

"Come on, Lotta," Linda Martinez said. "I'll show you your nice bedroom. I put a nice new spread on the bed and new curtains. And you can look out your window and see my husband's cute garden with elves and little bunny rabbits and foxes. There's a little fountain too."

"I don't want to go in that stinking house," Carlotta said, folding her arms and standing at the door.

"Lotta," Felix said, "you go in that front door, or so help me I'll throw you over my shoulder like a sack of potatoes and take you in."

Shock gripped the girl's face. She always considered Felix Martinez to be a monster, some creature from the netherworld that her crazy Aunt Linda had insanely married in a weak moment. But Mr. Martinez's threat worked. She entered the house.

"You don't still have that hideous dog, do you?" Carlotta asked.

"Yeah," Felix Martinez said. "Be nice to him, Lotta. He can tell if somebody doesn't like him. Makes him mad. No tellin' what he'll do."

Brutus sauntered out from his favorite spot under the kitchen table when he heard the strange voice. He looked at Carlotta and then hurried back under the table.

"Even *he* gets it," Mr. Martinez muttered.

Naomi looked up from the computer and said, "Hello, Carlotta." She knew her mother would have liked her to say, "Nice to see you, Carlotta," or "I hope you'll be happy here," but all those pleasantries stuck in Naomi's throat.

Carlotta stared at Naomi. "I h-hate being here," she stammered.

Naomi thought to herself, "Not anymore than I hate you being here, Carlotta. I'd rather the Creature From the Black Lagoon was moving into Zack's old bedroom." But Naomi forced herself to say, "It'll get better."

Linda Martinez looked at her daughter gratefully. She knew how Naomi felt, and she was so proud of her daughter that she wasn't letting her feelings overcome courtesy.

"Come on, honey," Mom said. "Let me show you the nice bedroom. It's all fresh and—"

"I don't want to see the ugly, horrible bedroom," Carlotta said, folding her arms defiantly and standing in the middle of the kitchen.

"Okeydokey," Felix Martinez said. "Looks like we gotta go to plan B, then. We'll move the suitcases out onto the porch, Lotta. You can sleep out there with Brutus.

You can use his doggy blankets. They sorta have a doggy smell to them, but you'll get used to it."

Carlotta's eyes widened in horror.

"Come on, Naomi, let's get her clothes out on the porch so it'll be handy for her," Felix Martinez said to his daughter. "Oh, Lotta, sometimes at night the opossums come and look in the slats of the porch, but don't mind them. They got these big teeth, but they're pretty harmless."

Carlotta quickly followed Linda Martinez down the hall to Zack's old bedroom.

Felix Martinez looked at Naomi and winked. In spite of what was happening, Naomi had to chuckle.

CHAPTER TWO

They had enrolled Carlotta Valencia at Cesar Chavez High School, so when Ernesto Sandoval came to pick up Naomi on Monday morning, Carlotta was waiting too.

Ernesto was expecting a girl with a pointy head and green, glowing eyes. But she was actually rather pretty, with an oval face and nice brown eyes. She was as tall as Naomi, but she did outweigh her. Naomi was wearing her skinny jeans and a soft blue pullover, and Carlotta was wearing jeans that cost three times more and that were skintight and screaming for more room. Carlotta did not look nearly as good as Naomi.

"Ernie," Naomi said, "this is my cousin,

Carlotta Valencia. She's staying with us for a while. Carlotta, this is my boyfriend, Ernesto Sandoval. He's senior class president, and one of the nicest guys in the school."

Carlotta gave Ernesto a long look. A tiny smile flickered on her lips. It was the first smile Naomi had seen on her cousin's face since she had arrived on Bluebird Street.

"Man, you're cute," Carlotta said to Ernesto.

"Thanks," Ernesto said, feeling uneasy. Naomi got into Ernesto's Volvo in the front seat, and Carlotta sat in back. Among the many negative things Naomi had told Ernesto about her cousin was that she was boy crazy. She flirted with every boy she saw unless he looked like an ogre.

"Is this your grandfather's car, Ernie?" Carlotta asked.

"No," Ernesto said. "It's mine. When I was sixteen, I really wanted a car, and this was the cheapest I could find. It's not very sporty, but it's reliable."

Carlotta looked out the window as

they drove. "This is such a horrible neighborhood. Where I live up north, Huntington Beach, it's so nice. This is the slums, right?" she said.

"No, it's the *barrio,*" Naomi said coldly, exchanging a look with Ernesto.

"Most of the people who live here don't have a lot of money," Ernesto said, "but they're good people for the most part. They try to keep up their houses."

"Our neighborhood in Huntington Beach, it's beautiful," Carlotta said. "I mean, we're Mexican Americans, but we didn't live in a community full of Latinos up there. Wow, everybody around here looks so ethnic. They look like they're poor." There was scorn in Carlotta's voice.

Ernesto was beginning to get the picture. "Carlotta," he said, "Latinos are just as good as anybody else. I have some wonderful friends at Chavez High who're all of Mexican descent. Most of our teachers are Mexican Americans, and they're great. I love it here."

"Look at all the graffiti," Carlotta said, wrinkling her nose. "Do the gangs do that?"

"Sometimes," Ernesto said, "or sometimes just kids trying to make a statement. We had a couple boys at Chavez who dropped out in their junior year and tagged all over the *barrio,* but their stuff was good. My father, he teaches at Chavez, he and some of us got the boys back in school, and now they're making money doing murals. They did a great mural on the side of a school building—you'll see it—it was covered by all the local TV stations. It's of Cesar Chavez and the farmworkers and Bobby Kennedy."

"Who was Cesar Chavez?" Carlotta asked. "I never heard of him. It seems weird to name a school after somebody nobody ever heard of."

Ernesto sighed. "He started a union for farmworkers in California and got them decent wages and safer working conditions," he said.

"He must have died fifty years ago or

something," Carlotta said, "because I've never heard of him."

"Well, he died in nineteen ninety-three," Ernesto said, "and most people *have* heard of him. California declared March thirty-first a legal holiday to celebrate his life, and the U.S. Post Office put out a stamp commemorating Chavez in two thousand and two."

They pulled into the parking lot of Cesar Chavez High School, and Carlotta got out. She looked around and said, "What an ugly school. Where I went to school in Orange County, we had beautiful green lawns, and it was sorta on a hill where you could see the ocean. Ugh, this is pitiful."

Naomi could take no more. "Well, Carlotta," she said in a malevolent voice, "you couldn't have been all that happy there or you wouldn't have called your principal a 'crazy old crone' and spit in her face and gotten expelled."

Carlotta turned to Ernesto and said, "Naomi has always been jealous of me.

Naomi knows my father makes a lot more money than her father, and we can afford a better life, so she likes to cut me down by saying mean things."

"Well," Ernesto said, "it's the truth, isn't it? That stuff did happen at your old school, right?"

"It wasn't my fault," Carlotta said. "The principal was a bitter old woman, and she was mad at how pretty I am, so she told my parents lies about me. She lied about me to the school trustees too, and that's why I had to leave."

Behind Carlotta's back, Ernesto rolled his eyes and Naomi grinned.

Naomi helped Carlotta with her class schedule, making sure she found all the classes she belonged in. The only class they shared was Mr. Jesse Davila's U.S. history class. After class, Carlotta said, "I didn't think guys that old were still allowed to teach."

"He's a very good teacher," Naomi said. "He worked for a while in the diplomatic service. A couple weeks ago, he got a woman who used to be secretary of state to visit the class on video conferencing. It was cool."

When Ernesto dropped Carlotta home at the Martinez house, he and Naomi remained in the Volvo talking.

"How'd it go, babe?" Ernesto asked. "I was thinking about you all day."

"I guess it went okay," Naomi said. "She doesn't like any of her teachers, but what else is new? She said they gave too much homework. But it wasn't as bad as I feared."

"Babe, I'm proud of you," Ernesto said. "I know how you feel, but you still really did your best for her today. You're a class act, Naomi."

"Oh, Ernie, I was burning up inside," Naomi said.

"But you pulled it off, babe," Ernesto said.

Ernesto gave Naomi a kiss, and they held it for as long as they could without encouraging someone in the Martinez house to start looking out. Then Naomi ran inside, waving Ernesto off.

"How was your first day at Chavez, sweetie?" Linda Martinez was asking Carlotta.

"Oh, it's a horrible school, but I managed. They've got this one old teacher who looks like he belongs in a nursing home. His name is Davila," Carlotta said.

"He's a fine teacher," Naomi cut in.

Felix Martinez was sitting in his chair reading the sports section of the newspaper. His favorite team had just traded away his favorite player, and he was in a bad mood anyway. He looked up and said, "Hey, Lotta, you ever been to one of these sausage factories, you know, where they put the meat into the casings?"

"No, I never have," Carlotta said. "That sounds disgusting."

"Well, you know what reminded me of that?" Mr. Martinez began to say.

"Felix! No!" Linda pleaded.

"Hey, I ain't gonna be shushed in my own house, lady. When something needs saying, I'm gonna say it. Lotta, when you wear those tight jeans that're too small for you, you look like those sausages, you know? The fat cells in your chubby legs are fighting against the denim."

Carlotta turned a dark shade of red. Her eyes filled with tears. "I'm not fat!" she cried.

"No, you're not, but you need to wear a bigger size jeans. Lot of teenage boys, they're like wolves drooling, you know. They see something like you sashayin' around in those too-small jeans, and you could get in trouble," Felix Martinez said.

Carlotta looked mortified, and Naomi's mother hurried to smooth things out. "I'm making something really nice for dinner, Lotta. I know you'll like it. Maple-glazed meatloaf. The family just loved it when I made it before."

"I hate meatloaf," Carlotta said. "It reminds me of dog food."

"Well, then maybe you can skip the meat-loaf and go out and eat with Brutus, what-ever he's gettin'," Mr. Martinez snapped.

Linda Martinez looked sick. "Carlotta, dear, this is delicious meatloaf with chopped onions and bell peppers, and what makes it extra special is the maple syrup glaze," she said.

"Yeah," Naomi said. "It's really good."

When they sat down to dinner, Carlotta glared at her plate and took out her cell phone. She began texting her friends in Huntington Beach, telling them what a nightmare she was going through.

"Hey, Lotta, knock it off," Naomi's father growled. "Rules of the house. We don't text during dinner."

"I'm not bothering anyone," Carlotta snapped, continuing to text.

"You're gonna stop texting until dinner is over, or I swear I'm gonna take that phone away from you, Lotta. You can text all your idiot friends after dinner," Felix Martinez said.

Carlotta put her phone away and began nibbling on the meatloaf. In spite of her determination to hate every bite, she liked it. She wouldn't admit it, but it was delicious. Carlotta's mother was not a very good cook, and they relied heavily on take-out. Carlotta was sick of that, but she would rather die than admit how good this meatloaf was. Carlotta didn't want to do or say anything that would give the Martinezes any indication that anything here pleased her.

Carlotta went to her room after dinner and curled up on the bed texting. Her closest friend at her old school, Katy, got her first text.

"Katy, this is like living in a horrible maximum security prison!"

Katy called back. "That bad, huh, Lotta?"

"Worse! Uncle Felix is an absolute fiend. He wouldn't let me text at dinner, and he's making fun of how I look in my jeans. And he threatened me, Katy. He says maybe I'll have to sleep on the porch with this vicious pit bull they got," Carlotta said.

"Oh, Lotta, you don't have to take that," Katy said. "Call your parents and tell them what's going on, and they'll come get you."

"No, they won't, Katy. They've turned against me. Mom and Dad hate me 'cause I embarrassed them at that private school. That horrible old Fenwick lied about me, and my parents sided with her. Mom and Dad love my sisters so much 'cause they fawn over our parents all the time. They're disgusting bootlickers. Ali and Maggie make me look bad 'cause I'm not always buttering our parents up. They've exiled me to this house of horror to punish me so much that they think I'll be like Ali and Maggie when I get home, licking their feet. That's what Mom and Dad want! Kids who worship them!"

"You poor thing," Katy said. "I feel so bad for you. What about that Naomi? Is she being a creep?"

"Oh man, yes. She's worse than I ever

imagined. Today was my first day at that ugly Cesar Chavez High where I'm stuck. I was all mixed up on my schedule, and Naomi wouldn't help me at all. I was on my own. She just hates me being here so much. She's always been jealous of me 'cause my family has more money and can buy me nicer clothes," Carlotta said.

"How awful," Katy said.

"Yeah, and they stuck me in this horrible little dinky bedroom, and when I look out the window, I see this grotesque garden that Uncle Felix made with little winged devils or something. It's so ugly. Aunt Linda said the carvings were elves, but they look more like devils to me, little twisted devils sitting on toadstools. I'm telling you, Katy, Uncle Felix is sick!" Carlotta said.

"Oh, Lotta, it sounds like you're trapped in a horror movie," Katy said.

"Yeah, exactly. Oh! I gotta go now. Aunt Linda is coming down the hall. She's such a wimp. She does everything her husband says. She's just pathetic. Okay, she's almost here, bye Katy." Carlotta tapped the End button on her phone.

"Is everything all right, dear?" Linda Martinez asked as she looked in the room. "You can watch TV on the little set there, or use that computer there. Felix is watching the game on the big TV, and you're welcome to join us. But we usually have lights out at eleven. Your uncle gets up early to go to the construction sites. He's a forklift operator, you know, and he works very hard."

"Eleven! The good talk shows just get started at eleven. I love the late-night talk shows. Back home, I'd watch them until like two a.m.," Carlotta said.

Felix Martinez came up behind his wife in the hall. "You know what, Lotta? Maybe that was why you were flunking on all your tests in that high-class private school, so's you had to go and cheat, 'cause you were up all night watching idiot talk shows. That ain't gonna get you nowhere. You do your homework, and then get some sleep so you can listen to what the teachers are sayin' in class," he said.

"It's not fair that my whole life is being turned upside down," Carlotta cried, tears starting to run down her face.

"You know what's not fair, Lotta?" Felix Martinez said, going past his wife and entering the girl's room.

"Felix! No!" Linda groaned.

"Go clean up the dishes, Linda," Mr. Martinez snapped. Then he turned to Carlotta. "What ain't fair is that we got a home here where everybody tries to do their best and nobody is whining and causin' trouble, and now we got a spoiled brat living with us, which we did not ask for."

Mr. Martinez continued complaining. "It's like you got a nice garden with daffodils and pansies and birds singing in the trees and a rattlesnake moves in. He scares off the birds and crawls around ruining the flowers. That's not fair. So you mind your p's and q's, girl. I'm not your father, and for that I thank the One upstairs, but as long as you're here, you do what I say. I'm not the pushover sap your father is. Behave yourself. I'm not that poor old Fenwick dame that you cussed out and spit at. You spit in my face, Lotta, I'll spit right back in your face."

"Felix," Linda groaned.

"You still here? I thought you were out with the dishes, lady. You think the dishes are gonna clean themselves?" Mr. Martinez went back to the living room where the game was winding up.

Naomi appeared in the doorway of Carlotta's room then. "You get your homework done already?" she asked.

"I always do it in the morning, before school," Carlotta said.

"It's only eight o'clock, Carlotta, why don't you do it now? Mr. Davila wants two pages on America's relationship with North Korea. It took me an hour to write mine," Naomi said.

Carlotta frowned. "When did he assign that? I didn't hear him say anything about North Korea. That old fool mumbled everything so it's no wonder nobody can get anything straight," she said.

"Lotta, he speaks very clearly, and we spent the whole class talking about North Korea. Don't you have anything in your notes about North Korea?" Naomi asked.

"I didn't take notes. I was uh … texting. I always sit in the back of the classroom so I don't bother anybody when I text," Carlotta said.

Naomi rolled her eyes. "You were texting during class? Oh, Lotta, don't do that! If Mr. Davila or any of the teachers see you doing that, you'll be in trouble," Naomi said. She opened her own binder and said, "These are the notes I took today. Read them over, and then maybe you could write something about America's problems with North Korea."

Naomi disliked Carlotta and wished with all her heart that she hadn't come to live here. Still, Naomi could not get past her own personality, which was programmed to be helpful, even to people who didn't deserve it. Naomi couldn't just smile to herself and relish the thought that Carlotta wouldn't have her assignment done, and she'd get an automatic F for that project tomorrow in class.

"Oh, okay," Carlotta said, glancing at the notes.

As Carlotta started to write her paper, she said, "Actually, I'm very smart. I took an intelligence test, and I was like eligible for Mensa. My mother said she was lots smarter than your mother when they were kids in school, so I guess that's why I'm so smart. It's in the blood or something. I can just skim something and write an A assignment."

"That's wonderful," Naomi said with sarcasm. "I get good grades, but I work for them. Speaking of that, you've got Samson for English, and I hope you're reading the short story she assigned. She's a bear if you come to class the next day and can't discuss the story. I had her last year, and I made sure I was always ready for the discussion."

"We were given some stupid Hemingway story," Carlotta said.

"Read it, Carlotta, or face the consequences," Naomi said. "You don't want to be on Samson's bad list." Naomi turned then. "Well, I gotta finish my math homework. See you in the morning."

Carlotta didn't thank Naomi for what she had just done. Instead, she started texting Katy again.

"It's getting worse. Not only is that ogre Uncle Felix on my case, but that witchy little Naomi is bossing me around now too. She was just in here, harassing me. I could just die!"

Carlotta lay on the bed then, thinking about the boys she'd seen today at school. There were some cute ones. Carlotta wondered how committed Ernie was to Naomi.

CHAPTER THREE

Naomi drove Carlotta to school the next day in her car. Carlotta was disappointed that Ernesto Sandoval didn't drive them again. All last night, Carlotta thought about that handsome dark-eyed, dark-haired boy who gave her goose bumps.

As the girls walked onto the campus, Carlotta said, "Who's *that* guy?"

"Clay Aguirre," Naomi said. Clay was walking alone. When she was a junior, Naomi had dated Clay, even though he was rude and abusive. Then she got smart and ditched him for Ernesto Sandoval. "He's a football player for the Cougars."

"Wow," Carlotta said, "he's hot!"

"He's got a steady girlfriend, Mira Nuñez. They're really close," Naomi said.

Carlotta shrugged. "Nothing to worry about. Boyfriends come and go in high school. I had six boyfriends in my school since I was in ninth grade. But I never had one as cute as that dude there. Look at those shoulders! Doesn't he just send you into orbit?" she said.

"No," Naomi said, though she had to admit he once did, before she found out what he was really like.

"He's in my English class with that creepy Samson," Carlotta said. "I saw him real quick yesterday, but I didn't notice how hot he was. I hate that class so much because Samson is sooo boring, but now that I've gotten a good look at Clay …"

"You know, Lotta, Clay and Mira really hang out all the time. She's crazy about him. If I were you, I wouldn't mess with him," Naomi said.

"She doesn't own him, does she?" Carlotta snapped. She turned and walked into Lydia Samson's class, leaving Naomi standing there staring after her.

One time Naomi's father had said there was bad blood in the Valencia family. It came from Carlotta's great-grandfather. He was mixed up in organized crime in the 1920s. He was sent to jail for a long time. Looking at Carlotta and seeing how little she seemed to care for other people, Naomi was tempted to buy that theory.

Ms. Samson was a severe-looking woman, about forty, with her washed-out blonde hair pulled back from her face. She wore a minimum of makeup. Everybody speculated that she led a lonely single life and that teaching was her only passion.

Clay Aguirre especially liked to make fun of Ms. Samson, suggesting that when she was in high school, she was in the "dog" category.

Now Carlotta changed seats from where she had sat the first day. Ms. Samson didn't assign seats. Carlotta found a seat right ahead of Clay, and she made sure she was standing in front of him in her tight jeans for several seconds. Mira Nuñez had not yet arrived in class.

"Whoa, nice view," Clay said with appreciation, his gaze pinned on the girl.

"Oh … thanks," Carlotta said, turning to him. "I heard you were the best football player in the school." Carlotta looked at him adoringly.

"I guess so," Clay said. "I sure helped the team almost get to the championships."

"I just love boys who play football," Carlotta cooed. "I think they look like brave warriors out there, fighting for the glory of the school. I think it's amazing that you guys spend so much time practicing and play that dangerous game. I think it's awesome."

Mira Nuñez arrived and took her usual seat beside Clay. She cast a dirty look at the girl who seemed to be carrying on a warm conversation with him. "Hi, Clay," Mira said.

"Hi, Mira," Clay said, but he continued talking to Carlotta. "Yeah, we athletes work hard and risk injury and not everybody appreciates it. We play through pain most games. Uh, what did you say your name was?"

"Carlotta Valencia. I'm from Huntington Beach, but right now I'm staying with my cousin Naomi Martinez, 'cause the family can use some help. They're not doing so well financially, and I'm helping with that," Carlotta said.

"Well, Carlotta," Clay said warmly, "can I call you Carly?"

"Sure, I like that," Carlotta said. "Carly sounds sweet."

Ms. Samson came into the classroom then, clad as she usually was in a dark pullover and a dark skirt. She wore no jewelry except for a gold chain with a pendant at the end. "I know you've all read *The Snows of Kilimanjaro,* which showed Hemingway in a crucial stage of his writing career. The story reflects his experience as a big-game hunter in Africa when he was only in his thirties. What important elements of his style are very much apparent here?"

Clay raised his hand, "Well, his kind of macho realism. He wasn't sentimental. I liked that."

"Yes," Ms. Samson said, "I assigned everyone to go online and find out what Hemingway's growing political views were at this time. So, what would we have to say about that?"

"Well," Mira Nuñez said, "he was getting left-wing. He was interested in the Spanish Civil War, and he was on the side of the Communists or loyalists."

"Do you agree with that, Carlotta?" Ms. Samson asked.

"Uh, no," Carlotta said, desperately grasping at straws. "Hemingway was a good American. He wouldn't have been with the Communists. That's just stupid."

"You didn't do the assignment, did you, Carlotta?" Ms. Samson asked harshly. She reminded Carlotta of Ms. Fenwick. "You didn't go online and look into Heming-way's views."

"I … just didn't have time," Carlotta

said. "I'm new here, and I don't think it's fair to expect me to be on top of everything. I just moved into a relative's house, and everything is chaos, and I'm expected to do the cleaning and everything."

Clay Aguirre spoke up then. "Yeah, Ms. Samson, we gotta cut the girl some slack."

Ms. Samson glared at Clay. "Thank you so much, Clay, for advising me how to run my classroom. I appreciate that. I have only been teaching for eighteen years," she said.

After class, Clay was talking to Carlotta as Mira watched from a distance. "Thanks for defending me, Clay," Carlotta said. "What a witch that teacher is."

"Well," Clay said, laughing, "she's a dried-up old spinster, and she's mad at the world, so she takes it out on her students, especially on cute chicks like you. Just hang in there, Carly. You'll be fine."

"Thanks again," Carlotta said. "You're as nice as you're hot!"

Clay threw back his head and laughed heartily. He was really enjoying this. At times like this, he almost regretted his commitment to Mira. But Clay did care about Mira. As Carlotta walked away, Clay spotted Mira standing there staring at him. She had a cold look on her face.

"Hey, Mira, how's it going?" he asked, as if nothing was wrong.

Mira drew closer and said, "What's going on, Clay?"

"What? Huh? I don't know what you mean, babe. I was trying to help out the new kid. Is that a problem for you?" Clay asked.

"Clay, if the new kid was a guy or a plain girl, you wouldn't have bothered with them. She's cute and a flirt, so you're eating up her sweet talk," Mira said in a hurt voice.

"Hey, babe, don't get all bent out of shape, okay? The poor kid probably comes from some dysfunctional family, and she's struggling. We gotta help each other out, right?" Clay said.

"That's a real new attitude for you, Clay," Mira snapped. "You sound like Ernie Sandoval, but it's sincere with him. He'd help a girl who looked like what you'd call a dog, with the same enthusiasm as if she was hot. Ernie is compassionate toward everybody, guys, girls, tall, short, cute, and homely. Seems like you only care for a chick whose jeans are so tight it's a wonder she can even sit down!"

"Whoa," Clay said, "the green-eyed monster has really got its teeth into you, babe." There was now anger in Clay's voice.

Ernesto and Naomi were standing nearby when the fight got loud. "Oh man," Naomi groaned. "Carlotta is causing trouble with those two! She was flirting with Clay, I bet, and now Mira is ticked off!"

Ernesto shook his head. "I feel sorry for Mira having to fight for Clay Aguirre. It's like fighting over a half-eaten drumstick."

"Aunt Mia told me that Carlotta had half the senior girls in that private school hating each other. She just flirted shamelessly with every boy, cutting in on every relationship," Naomi said.

Abel Ruiz came along. "Hey, Naomi,

did she steal a pair of your jeans? Those seams are crying for mercy," he said.

"She wears all her clothes tight on purpose," Naomi said. "She says that's the best guy bait there is. Dad had this big fight with her over that. He tried to shame her into getting a bigger size, but it didn't work."

"Good for your dad," Ernesto said.

"You know," Abel said, "she'll be after you pretty soon, Ernie. I don't have to worry. With my looks, she's gonna look right past me, but I've already seen her drooling over you."

"Come on, Abel," Ernesto said. "Cassie down at the Sting Ray thinks you're plenty hot. As far as her coming after me, boy is she mining a dead hole. She's got as much chance with me as a snowball in hell."

"You guys," Naomi said, "I hate to have to break this to you, but Carlotta will probably be eating lunch with us today under the trees. I hate to do that to you, but the little jerk will be eating alone if we don't."

48

"That's okay, Naomi," Abel said. "When she steals Clay away from Mira, then those two can go and eat on the stone bench where Clay and Mira usually eat. Then we'll be rid of her. Actually, that'd be a good thing. Mira deserves better than Clay, and it looks like Carlotta and Clay sorta deserve each other."

"Poor Mira would be heartbroken, though," Naomi said. "She really loves Clay."

"Better heartbroken now than a fat lip down the road," Abel said.

"Maybe he wouldn't hit Mira like he did me," Naomi said. "Maybe he's grown or learned something. I don't know."

Abel shook his head. "Guys don't change. Chicks either. We just go on and on making the same mistakes till the undertaker shovels dirt on us," he said.

At lunchtime, Naomi brought Carlotta down to the spot under the trees where Ernesto, Abel, Carmen, Bianca, Julio, and Mona Lisa were already opening their lunch bags.

Naomi introduced her cousin to those who hadn't met her yet.

"So, how's it going so far, Carlotta?" Ernesto asked between bites of his peanut butter and jelly sandwich.

"Oh, it's hard," Carlotta groaned, "to come to a new school in the middle of my senior year. I still can't believe this is happening to me. I had so many friends at my school. I was so looking forward to graduating with all my friends. But my parents pulled me out."

"What happened to screw things up for you?" Julio asked.

"Uh, well, there was this horrible principal at the school who just hated me. She made up all kinds of lies about me and, well, like this old hag told my parents that I cheated on my tests and stuff, so she got me expelled from school. My parents thought it'd be better if I made a fresh start down here," Carlotta said.

But Julio would not let the matter rest. He had a mean streak, and he figured this girl was lying through her teeth. He sensed that Carlotta Valencia was not a nice human being. "If you got expelled, then you couldn't have graduated with your friends, and it wasn't your parents' fault, right?" he said.

"But they didn't fight for me, and they should have," Carlotta said. "They believed this old hag." A faint smile came to Carlotta's lips then. "But something good did happen this morning. I was in Ms. Samson's class, she's horrible like the witch who expelled me, but a really sweet boy came to my defense. Ms. Samson was ripping me, and he stepped right up and made her stop. His name is Clay Aguirre, and he's cute and he plays football—"

"He's the worst creep in the school," Julio Avila said matter-of-factly. "If there was a likability contest between him and a black widow spider, the black widow spider would win."

Mona Lisa Corsella, Julio's girlfriend for the past several weeks, laughed so hard she almost choked on her sandwich. Julio had the reputation for being a kind of bad boy because he never pulled his punches, but he was a very good guy deep down. Mona Lisa was growing to like him more each day.

Carlotta looked shocked, "How can you say such a thing about Clay? He seemed so nice," she gasped.

"Because it's the truth," Ernesto said before Julio could answer. "Julio has this bad habit of speaking the truth. It doesn't always make him popular, but he's one of my favorite homies. He's the kind of homie you want in a pinch."

Mona Lisa smiled and squeezed Julio's arm. When she foolishly ran away from home and ended up stranded in Phoenix, Arizona, Julio drove there to bring her home.

"Clay is going with Mira Nuñez anyway," Carmen said, looking at Carlotta with less than admiration. "It's not cool to get ideas about another chick's dude."

"Oh, I don't think he likes her that much,"

Carlotta said, tossing her head. "I mean, the way I see it, girls or women don't steal guys from chicks the guys are real happy with, you know what I mean? If Clay liked this Mira chick all that much, he wouldn't have come on so strong to me. It's like she's not giving him what he needs."

Bianca Marquez was in therapy for anorexia, and she was eating one of the sandwiches Abel Ruiz made for her. Abel and Bianca hung out a lot, but neither of them were deeply into the relationship. They were just very good friends. Bianca loved the delicious sandwiches Abel made for her, and she looked over at Ernesto eating his peanut butter and jelly sandwich. "Ernie, how can you stand eating peanut butter and jelly all the time? Don't you get sick of it?"

"Yeah," Ernesto said, "but Mom is so busy writing her books that she hasn't got time to pack anything else for me and my sisters. There's leftover ham and turkey in the fridge, but I never know when it's gonna be a hot day, and the sandwich will go bad and poison me or something. The good thing about peanut butter and jelly is that it never goes bad."

Naomi was giggling as Ernesto seriously explained his strategy. She listened to him, her eyes overflowing with the love she felt for him.

"I sorta vary my peanut butter and jelly sandwiches too," Ernesto said. "I'll have grape jelly one day and raspberry the next, or apple butter, so they're not all exactly the same. Sometimes I'll use creamy peanut butter and sometimes crunchy," Ernesto acknowledged.

Abel, Bianca, Naomi, Carmen, and Mona Lisa were laughing, but Carlotta looked annoyed. She didn't see anything funny about Ernesto and his peanut butter sandwiches, though she continued to think he was awfully hot, and if things didn't work out between her and Clay, Ernesto was a distinct possibility for her next efforts.

"Clay and I have that ugly Ms. Samson

for English," Carlotta said, wanting to change the subject from peanut butter and jelly sandwiches. "And she's so awful. She never smiles or makes jokes. She dresses in black like a witch. Clay explained to me why she's so awful. She's pretty ugly, and she must have been ugly when she was a teen-ager so no guys would date her, and that's why she's so bitter. I could tell right away that she didn't like me 'cause, you know, I look pretty good, and naturally she's gonna hate the better-looking girls even more because—"

"I had her last year, and I liked her," Carmen said. Carmen was beginning to regard Carlotta as a pain in the neck. "She's pretty popular with the students because she makes classes interesting."

Carlotta ignored that completely. She said, "Clay hit the nail on the head, I think. She's so mean-spirited because she's had a loveless life, the poor wretch."

"That sounds just like what that low-life Aguirre would say," Julio said. "Like he has any idea of what Ms. Samson's life has been like. He always does that. He runs down people he doesn't know anything about because it makes the mean little cockroach feel good about himself to drag other people down. From what I've heard, Ms. Samson is a darn good teacher, and she doesn't look half bad either. When she was a young chick, I bet she had lots of boyfriends."

"You're right, Julio," Bianca said. "I was looking in the yearbooks from Cesar Chavez High, and I found one the year she started teaching here. She was very pretty. She's been teaching here almost twenty years."

Ernesto had been listening quietly, and now he said, "It's a mistake to assume stuff about people, Carlotta. We don't know what Ms. Samson's life has been like. It's none of our business, and we shouldn't specu- late. She might be carrying sorrows in her heart that none of us could dream of. Just do the assignments she asks for, Carlotta, and you'll get a good grade. She's a very fair grader. My friend Dom Reynosa was in her class last year, and he's not good in English, but he tried really hard. He ended up with a B, his first B in English. I like her for what she did for Dom, making him stretch like he never did in English before."

Carlotta seemed offended. She left early. Julio applauded when she was gone.

CHAPTER FOUR

Naomi always enjoyed playing her favorite music during her short drive to school in her car, but Carlotta, now her passenger whether she liked it or not, didn't like the same music, so another of Naomi's tiny pleasures was gone.

"Wow, this is such a cool car, Naomi," Carlotta said as they pulled onto the school campus. "Look, two guys are looking at us! They're pretty hot-looking too. You're so lucky, Naomi, to have a car like this. When did your parents buy it for you? Last year?"

"They didn't buy it for me," Naomi said. "I work part time, and I saved enough money to buy the car."

"Oh. Well, my mean parents won't

even let me have a car. Your parents are kinda poor, so I see why you had to pay for it yourself, but my parents are rich. They could easily get me a car. They didn't because they don't really care about me," Carlotta confessed.

"Do you have a driver's license, Carlotta?" Naomi asked.

"I did have one," Carlotta said. "I passed the written test real easy, and I went riding with the guy, and it was great. I got my license right away, when I was sixteen."

"Yeah," Naomi said, "that's when I got mine. It was one of the happiest days of my life."

"But I lost mine," Carlotta said. "It was so unfair."

"You *lost* it?" Naomi asked. "Why didn't you go down to the DMV and get a replacement? They'll—"

"No, see, Mom let me drive her Toyota right after I got my license, and I had a little accident, and Mom had a hissy fit just because it cost so much … I mean, like the car was totaled, but it didn't look that bad to me. I had the green light, and I made a left turn in front of some maniac who didn't stop, and he came barreling through. The stupid cop said it was my fault, some mumbo jumbo about drivers making a left turn being always at fault or stuff. And then there were a couple of other little tickets, and they took my license away," Carlotta said.

"It was so unfair because I'm an excellent driver. I don't have a license now, but the cops almost never stop you to see the license, so what's the difference? So maybe once in a while I could borrow your car, just for a little spin around town."

"Lotta, don't go there," Naomi said emphatically. "Don't even try to go there. The day I loan my car to somebody who doesn't have a license is the day Brutus is elected to the state senate."

"Well, you don't have to be nasty about it," Carlotta spat.

"Carlotta, I've got to say this, and I

hope you won't take offense. We all make mistakes. I've made some, and I owned them. I've done stupid things, and I admit it. But nothing that happens to you is *ever* your fault, do you know that? Somebody else was being mean or stupid or unfair whenever something bad happened to you. Where is that coming from? If we don't own our mistakes, then we don't learn from them, you know?" Naomi said.

"I always knew you hated me," Carlotta spat. "I don't know why, but I could feel that you hated me ever since we were little kids. I guess it was jealousy 'cause I had better clothes and nicer toys. I lived high on a hill in a beautiful house, and you lived here in the slums."

"This isn't the slums, and I've never hated you," Naomi said. "The people around here struggle to pay their bills, but we had very few foreclosures even when things were awful. I'm proud of my neighborhood, and I wouldn't want to live in Huntington Beach."

"Naomi, why don't you come clean? How can you like that dinky little house you live in with that horrible garden your father made full of carved devils?" Carlotta said. "I mean, those hideous little devils sit on mushrooms and stare at the smelly green pond."

"Dad's little garden is beautiful, Lotta, and they are not devils on the mushrooms. They're cute little elves, and the pond is fresh and clean. We all enjoy sitting out there. Even when guests come, it's their favorite spot."

The only thing that Carlotta said that was true was that Naomi did not like her. She was fighting against the feeling of hatred that sometimes rose in her. Naomi had never liked her. Carlotta was selfish and mean and often hateful. What was there to like?

Before they left to go home that day, Naomi said, "Oh, Lotta, I forgot to tell you. Today is Friday, and we get assigned our chores on Friday. Dad puts the assignment list on the fridge. I don't want you to be surprised."

"The chores?" Carlotta gasped. "What are you talking about? What is your house? A slave labor camp? My parents are paying for my room and board, and I don't have to be a slave too!"

"Carlotta, ever since I was little kid, I had chores, my brothers too. It's just being part of a family. Dad writes them down, and everything goes smoothly. It's no big deal. Mop the kitchen floor, clean the bathrooms, dust the living room, feed the dog, stuff like that," Naomi said.

"I've never done stuff like that in my life!" Carlotta cried. "At home, we hire people to do that!"

Naomi pulled into the Martinez driveway and parked the car. Felix Martinez was finishing the front lawn and was now gathering clippings for the green-waste trash barrel.

"Hey, Naomi, Lotta," Mr. Martinez said in a fairly cheerful voice. "Your mother wants some bulbs planted, Naomi. You know, for the springtime and all that. I got them in the bed of my pickup. You girls want to change into your grungies and come out and help me stick them in the ground?"

"I don't have any grungies," Carlotta said coldly.

"Naomi will loan you some of hers," Naomi's father said, his voice slightly less cheerful.

"I hate working in the soil," Carlotta said. "The stuff ruins my fingernails. It takes me forever to get my hands looking normal again."

"I'll be waiting," Felix Martinez said. "Ten minutes. I want to get the bulbs in before dinnertime." His eyes were narrow with impatience. It was not a good sign.

Naomi and Carlotta went inside and changed into old jeans and tee shirts. They belonged to Zack. "These are nice and big and comfy," Naomi said.

"They're horrible and stiff," Carlotta wailed. "I've *never* worn boy clothes!"

"Well, there's a first time for everything," Naomi said with an evil glint in her eyes.

As they walked outside, Carlotta said, "I hate this so much. These clothes are so ugly. I feel like a horrible homeless person. Your father has no right to expect me to do this, like a miserable peon!"

"Please, Lotta, just go with the flow. If we work together, we'll be done in no time. Don't make Dad angry. Once he gets angry, the whole evening is ruined for everybody," Naomi said.

Naomi led the way to the pickup, collecting the bags of bulbs.

"Put 'em in right," Felix Martinez said. "Naomi, make sure she puts them in the right way. If you bury them with the wrong end sticking up, they don't come up."

"I know, Dad," Naomi said. "Come on, Lotta, we plant them in this space here, alongside the lawn. It looks so pretty in the springtime when the tulips and paperwhites come up."

"I'm not going to kneel on the filthy walk," Carlotta said. "It's all muddy."

"Please, Carlotta," Naomi said in a tight little voice. "Just kneel down in Zack's old jeans. When we're done, you can take them off and shower. For crying out loud, Lotta, don't make a federal case over some tulip bulbs!"

"Hey," Felix Martinez said, coming over. "Is the little princess getting upset 'cause somebody wants her to do a little work?"

"I just don't think it's fair when my parents are paying for my room and board to expect me—" Carlotta snarled.

"Listen up, you, Princess Pickle-Face," Mr. Martinez said. "There ain't enough money in the world to make up for having you in my house. Your aunt is a sap, and I'm letting you ruin our lives like this for her sake. You talk about fair? Life ain't fair, Princess Pickle-Face. Nice boys and girls are homeless and living in cheap motels or sleeping in cars 'cause their parents lost their jobs. Nice kids are going to bed hungry, and a selfish twit like you is making a fuss over ten minutes of honest work. Well, Princess Pickle-Face, you plant the bulbs like Naomi is doing, or you don't get no dinner tonight. Understand?"

Carlotta and Naomi got all the bulbs planted in ten minutes, and then they headed in the house. Carlotta's eyes were filled with angry tears, and her lower lip was quivering with outrage.

"Oh, Carlotta, dear," Linda Martinez said when she saw her, "What's the matter?"

Felix Martinez was right behind the girls. "Knock it off there, Linda. Don't go baby-ing Princess Pickle-Face here. Bad enough you let our boys get away with murder, and now they got no respect for their own father. Only by the mercy of the Lord they turned out fairly good and ain't in jail. Kids need discipline. Only reason we're stuck right now with her nasty behavior is 'cause your sister and her husband were afraid to disci-pline her. I asked the spoiled one to dirty up her pretty little pinkies planting some tulip bulbs, and you'd think I pulled her hair out, which I would like to do."

Carlotta headed for her room to strip off the grungies, and Naomi followed her to collect them. "Your father is a monster, Naomi," she cried.

"He's not a monster," Naomi said. "He's just a tough dad, and I love him very much."

Carlotta pulled off the clothes and cast them away from herself as if they were covered with leeches. She dashed into the bedroom and showered for what seemed like forever to cleanse all traces of her ordeal before she put on her own clothes. Then, she got on the phone to gripe.

"Oh, Katy," she groaned, "today was the worst day ever. My classes are all horrible, and my English teacher is a fiend. She made fun of me in front of the whole class. Naomi's evil father made me put on these filthy clothes and slave out in the yard for *hours*. The only thing that made today bearable was that cute guy, Clay Aguirre. I think he's falling for me. I'm so excited. He has a girlfriend, but I think he's ready to dump her for me."

"Oh, wow," Katy said. "That's cool."

"Naomi is being so nasty, Katy. She yelled at me in the car coming home from school, and she won't let me borrow her car even once. She said I was a bad driver, the little twit! Oh, but her father—he's the absolute worst. I think he's a devil. He's got these bushy eyebrows, and his eyes are fiery, like hot coals. I don't think he's human. I think he's like that guy in the horror movie—you know that Mr. Jekyll and Dr. Hyde? You know how he turned into a wild beast?"

"That was *Dr.* Jekyll and *Mr.* Hyde," Katy said.

"Whatever," Carlotta said. "Anyway, my mother is gonna call tonight, and I think when I tell her all this, she'll come get me for sure. I'm glad I haven't unpacked all the suitcases. I may be out of here tonight."

Mia Valencia called a few minutes later. "Now that you're all settled, how is it going, darling?" she asked.

"Oh, Mom, it's unbearable. You gotta come get me. Naomi is lording it over me. She's so nasty. It's like she's queen, and I'm her slave. Today she made me put on horrid dirty clothes and work in the garden. And Uncle Felix, he's like a mean devil. My fingernails are all broken and dirty and, Mom … please."

"It'll be better later on, darling," Mrs. Valencia said. "Every beginning is hard."

"No, Mom, it's getting worse. My teachers at that rotten broken-down school, they all hate me, and the whole neighborhood is full of wild gangbangers who put graffiti everywhere," Carlotta ranted on.

"Well, you must try harder to please your teachers, sweetheart," Carlotta's mother said. "I'm sure they'll come around."

"Mom, listen to me. Uncle Felix made a garden in the backyard full of little carved devils because—" Carlotta cried.

"Sweetheart, I've been in that garden, and those are sweet little elves sitting on toadstools, and then there are bunny rabbits and squirrels and that nice little pond," Mia Valencia said. "I've been trying to get your father to put something like that in our backyard."

"Mom, they're devils!" Carlotta almost screamed.

"No, they're the seven dwarves, I think. You know, Sleepy and Dopey and Sneezy and Doc, and now who am I forgetting?" Carlotta's mother said. "Oh yes, Bashful and—"

"Mommmmm," Carlotta screamed.

"And Grumpy. That's the one I always forget. And Happy, of course." Mrs. Valencia sounded very happy herself.

"Mom, you've got to—" Carlotta cried.

"I'll call you tomorrow, sweetheart," her mother said before she disconnected the call.

After dinner, Naomi led Carlotta to the refrigerator where the chores were listed.

"Oh, Lotta, you got it easy. You just need to feed Brutus and make sure he has fresh water. I got to mop the kitchen floor," Naomi said.

"I hate that dog! I'm terrified of him," Carlotta cried. "I'm not going near him."

"Lotta, look at Brutus sleeping there under the table. He's as gentle as a lamb. Look at that peaceful face. He's the most lovable dog I ever saw. All you need to do is open the little key on top of the can and dump his food into his dish and give him fresh water. That'll take about two minutes in the morning," Naomi said.

"Ohhh, this is so unfair," Carlotta cried.

"Well," Naomi said, "I gotta get ready for tonight. Me and Ernie are going out."

"You are so lucky," Carlotta groaned. "You've got a handsome boyfriend, and you can go on dates. But I'm trapped here like a prisoner. It's not fair. I didn't do anything to deserve this."

"Lotta, I bet you went on plenty of dates up in Huntington Beach," Naomi said.

"Yeah, and my parents ruined every one of them. I had to be home by two in the morning. *One time* I didn't get in until five a.m., and they went ballistic. It wasn't even my fault. My boyfriend got stopped for DUI, and he was taken away. I had to find a way to get home!" Carlotta cried. "And they grounded me for two weeks!"

"Wow," Naomi said. "If I got stranded with a drunken boyfriend, I think my parents would've grounded me until I turned eighteen!" Naomi tried to give Carlotta a pleasant smile. "Ernie and I promised my folks we'd be home by midnight tonight, and we will be. And you'll find a nice guy at Chavez, and then you can go out too."

"Naomi, do you think Clay Aguirre likes me?" Carlotta asked.

"I don't know. He's pretty solid with Mira," Naomi said. "They've been going together for months. There are lots of boys at Chavez nicer than Clay anyway."

"That Julio Avila is pretty cute, but I can tell he hates me," Carlotta said.

Naomi thought to herself, "That's putting it mildly."

That night, around eight, Carlotta's cell phone rang. She had slipped Clay Aguirre her number in class and told him to call her anytime.

"Carly?" a boy's voice asked.

"Yeah," Carlotta said, her heart racing. It sounded like Clay Aguirre, but she wasn't sure. "Is this Clay?"

"Yeah," he said. "How are you doin'?"

"Oh, I'm stranded here. I'm so lonely and depressed I could just die," Carlotta said.

"How about if I came over and maybe we can go to Hortencia's—that's a cool hangout near here. We could have some tacos and talk," Clay said.

"Oh, Clay, that would be so amazing! Oh, do you think Naomi's father would let us do that? He's so mean and vicious. He's a regular devil. He's the most evil man I ever met," Carlotta wailed. The thought that some wonderful, exciting diversion

was offering itself to her—and that Felix
Martinez would forbid it—was tearing her
apart. "I'm so afraid of him, Clay."

Clay Aguirre laughed. "Nahh, I know the
guy. He likes me. We're pals. Mr. Martinez
and I go way back. I used to date Naomi,
you know, but that weasel Ernesto Sandoval
got her away from me. But Felix's cousin
Monte Esposito was trying to keep his seat
on the council when that monkey Emilio
Ibarra was running against him. I worked
hard for Felix's cousin, and he really appreciated that. When I dated Naomi, I was
over at the house all the time, and Felix
and Linda treated me like one of their sons.
Hang tight, babe, and I'll be over in fifteen
minutes."

"Oh, Clay, that's wonderful. Oh, I
feel like I've been rescued from the pit of
despair," Carlotta said. After she ended the
call, she raced to the closet and picked out
something really pretty, a green embroi-
dered top and her smallest skinny jeans.
She had to struggle to get into them, but it

was worth it. Clay Aguirre would surely appreciate the result.

In about twenty minutes, Clay Aguirre pulled into the Martinez driveway in his Hyundai Equus, the expensive new car his parents had just bought for him. He was truly hated around Cesar Chavez High for driving a car that was worth more than about twenty of the beaters the other students were driving.

Felix Martinez saw Clay from the window, and he swung open the door. "Hey, kid, nice to see you," he said. "You're looking good, Clay. You did a bang-up job this year on the football field. If those other Cougars had half the talents and drive you got, we'd have made it to the championships."

Clay came in and said, "Thanks, Mr. Martinez. I met your niece Carlotta at school. We got to talking, and I thought it would be nice if I took her over to Hortencia's for a couple hours. Would that be okay with you?"

Felix laughed. "Well, Clay, I'm gonna be honest with you. The little twit is my wife's niece, and I can't stand her for sour apples, but if you got the stomach to take her out, more power to you. I call her Princess Pickle-Face, and the thought of her being out of my house for a couple hours is a joy to behold. So good luck, Clay," Mr. Martinez said.

CHAPTER FIVE

Carlotta rushed into the living room, overjoyed by her good luck.

"You have a nice time, honey," Linda Martinez said, relieved that her niece at last looked happy. It would be the first time since she arrived here.

"If she gets to be too much for you, Clay," Felix Martinez said, "just throw her in the trunk and bring her home. We'll understand."

Clay and Carlotta hurried out the door, and Carlotta was euphoric. It was as if she'd been trapped in a dungeon with spiders spinning webs in her hair and now, suddenly, her knight in shining armor had come to rescue her.

"Oh, Clay, is this beautiful new car really yours?" Carlotta gasped.

"All mine, babe," Clay laughed.

"Oh, Clay, you must have a wonderful part-time job to afford a car like this. You got school, football practice, and still you earn enough to—" Carlotta raved.

"No, I don't work. My parents bought me the car. My folks want me to concentrate on school and sports. That's important for me at this stage. I got really cool parents. They do everything for me. Never hassle me."

"Wow, Clay, you are so lucky," Carlotta said. "My parents are awful. Just because I made a few mistakes, they are punishing me by making me finish my senior year living with my aunt and uncle. Aunt Linda is okay, but Uncle Felix is so mean. I always hated him, and now I'm a prisoner in that horrible house."

"Well, I've always gotten along with Mr. Martinez," Clay said. "He's an interesting guy. He's got this hot temper, but you can get on his good side if you play up to him. I always tell him what a good father he is and stuff. I butter him up. He's got this lousy job as a forklift operator, and it's getting tougher as he gets older. Just try to be nice to him, Carlotta. A little sugar goes a long way."

"Well, I hate being a hypocrite, but I'll try, Clay," Carlotta said. She looked over at the young man's chiseled profile, and she thought he was just about the most handsome guy she'd ever seen. "Clay, did you and Naomi really date for a long time?

"Yeah, we did," Clay said.

"What happened? I mean to lose a guy like you must have broken her heart," Carlotta said.

Clay smiled. "Everybody at school knows what happened. No sense in lying about it. She dumped me for Ernesto Sandoval, that jerk. Talk about being a hypocrite, he's the biggest one at Chavez. He's so charming and stuff. Fools everybody. I'm a more down-to-earth guy. I say what I mean, and I mean what I say. When something is going on that I don't like, I speak up. Naomi didn't like that. She wants all sweetness and light. She gets her feelings hurt real easy, and I wasn't about to treat her like a queen."

"I don't like Naomi," Carlotta said. "She doesn't like me either. There's always been bad blood between us. She acts like she cares about me, and she tries to help me with my homework, but that's not sincere. She just likes to act like she knows everything and I'm stupid."

"Yeah, that sounds like her," Clay said.

They parked at Hortencia's, and Clay said, "We'll just have some flan and Mexican chocolate. I've eaten dinner already, and you probably did too."

"That sounds terrific," Carlotta said. "It's so wonderful just to get out of that house. Aunt Linda tries to stand up for me, but she's so under Uncle Felix's thumb."

They found a cozy little booth in the back, and soon the flan and frothy chocolate were on the table.

"The place is crowded," Carlotta said.

"Yeah. Hortencia serves the best Mexican food in the whole *barrio*. Word gets around. Everybody eats here," Clay said.

"I see a couple girls there who're in my English class," Carlotta said. "I don't know their names. They're not very friendly."

"Yeah, that's Tish and Loni," Clay said.

"Why are they staring at us like that?" Carlotta asked. "It's like their eyeballs are falling out of their heads."

Clay Aguirre suddenly seemed a little upset. He ate his flan hurriedly and drank the hot chocolate more quickly than he intended to. "I just remembered that I needed to finish a paper for history," he said. "I guess I gotta cut this short, babe. Sorry."

Carlotta finished her flan and smiled. "Oh, Clay, it's okay. Just getting out of the house even for a little while was heavenly, especially with a good-looking guy like you!"

Clay smiled faintly, and they went out to the Hyundai and headed back to Bluebird

Street. Before Carlotta got out of the car at her house she said, "Thanks, Clay. You really lifted my spirits."

"Yeah, it was fun," he said. But he looked preoccupied.

"You can call anytime, Clay," Carlotta said hopefully.

"Yeah, I might," he said. When Carlotta got to her door, she turned to wave at Clay, but he had already backed out of the driveway and was headed down the street.

"Did you have a nice time, dear?" Aunt Linda asked when Carlotta came in.

"Yeah, Clay is a cool guy. We just had some flan and Mexican chocolate, but it was good. Clay said Hortencia's is the hot spot around here. We were gonna hang out longer, but then Clay remembered he had to finish a school paper." It dawned on Carlotta then that today was Friday, and she wondered why Clay was in such a hurry when the paper wouldn't be due until Monday.

Clay noticed that those girls had been looking at them, and he seemed to change.

Carlotta couldn't figure it out.

"Naomi and Ernie are going to make a big night of it," Aunt Linda said. "They won't be home until midnight."

"Yeah," Carlotta said. She wanted to say something negative about Naomi, but she couldn't very well say it to Naomi's mother.

"I really like Clay, Aunt Linda," Carlotta said. "I think he likes me too. I hope he calls me again. If I had a boyfriend like him, it'd be so cool. He's just amazing."

Linda Martinez got a strange look on her face. She glanced around the corner to see what her husband was doing. He had started watching a crime show on TV, but then he did what he often did while he watched television, he fell asleep in his chair.

"Lotta," Linda Martinez said softly. "Naomi used to date Clay Aguirre."

"Yes, I know," Carlotta said. "Naomi told me and Clay did too."

Her voice very low, Linda Martinez said, "Your Uncle Felix likes Clay very

84

much, but I don't. When he dated Naomi, he was often rude to her, very rude. It hurt me to see her take that. And then one day, he slapped her in the face, leaving a bad bruise. It just broke my heart. I just wanted you to know, Lotta, that this boy has a side to him that isn't very nice. He may have gotten over that, but I wanted you to know."

"Well," Carlotta said, "thanks for telling me, but I don't think he'd ever do that to me. He just couldn't have been nicer tonight." Carlotta secretly thought that perhaps Naomi deserved to be smacked in the face. It amused Carlotta to know that something like that had happened to Naomi. It didn't make Carlotta think any less of Clay.

Right after her friend Tish called from Hortencia's, Mira Nuñez called Clay Aguirre.

Clay was just pulling into his driveway when his cell phone rang.

"Clay, I need to see you," Mira said in a terse voice.

Clay had been on edge all the way home tonight. Tish and Loni were close friends of Mira's. When Clay saw them in Hortencia's, he knew there would be trouble. "Yeah, babe, what's up?" he said in a casual voice.

"You know what's up," Mira said sharply. "Tish and Loni saw you chatting up some little twit at Hortencia's. That Carlotta chick who's staying with the Martinezes."

"Oh, that was nothing," Clay said. "Mr. and Mrs. Martinez asked me to take her out for an hour 'cause she's so depressed. I was just doing them a favor. I didn't want to, but Felix Martinez has always treated me right, and it was like doing something charitable."

"That's not like you, Clay. I saw you in English with your eyes bugging out staring at Carlotta's backside. You see a chick in tight clothes and you're off and running. Well, I've been through too much with you, Clay. You make a choice. You stop hanging around with her or don't come near my door anymore. You hear what I'm saying? I'm not kidding. I've been your sweet forgiving girlfriend for too long, but if you're gonna do stuff like this, then we're over," Mira's voice was hard and bitter. "I mean it!"

Clay was shocked by Mira's anger. She wasn't that kind of a girl. She was sweet and refined. And the truth was: Clay *did* love her. When he saw Carlotta, he thought it would be fun to have a little fling with her, just for laughs. Carlotta was hot, and he enjoyed her gushing compliments. But he never thought he was risking his relationship with Mira Nuñez. If he'd thought that, he wouldn't have gone near Carlotta.

"Mira, I swear, I just wanted to do a good turn for the Martinezes. Carlotta don't mean a thing to me. I love you, babe. I've told you that, and I mean it. This chick … she came on to me big-time, I admit it. But it didn't mean anything to me. Monday at school, I'll tell her to bug off, Mira," Clay said.

"Well, okay, Clay," Mira said. "I just don't want to be played for a fool."

Carlotta called Katy and told her all about the date with Clay. "For the first time since I've been here, Katy, something really wonderful happened. I think me and Clay are gonna be together a lot."

When Carlotta finished talking to Katy, her cell rang.

"Hey, Carly," Clay said. "It's Clay."

Carlotta's heart raced. She was expecting he'd call for another date but not this soon! "Oh, Clay. It's so good to hear your voice. I really enjoyed—"

"Hold on," Clay cut in. "You know those two chicks who were staring at us in Hortencia's? Those chicks from school? Well, they ratted me out, girl. They called my girlfriend, Mira Nuñez, and got her all steamed up that I was cheating on her."

"Oh, Clay, that's terrible," Carlotta said.

"Yeah, 'cause me and Mira got a good thing going. I don't want to mess that up. I was going to wait until Monday and talk to you then, but I got to thinking that this has got to be nipped in the bud sooner.

Hortencia's was fun tonight, and you're a hot chick, Carly. If it wasn't for Mira, maybe I'd be calling you again real soon, but I promised Mira I'd put a stop to this before anything else went down. So don't be hanging around me at school. Just ignore me, Carly. Thanks."

He hung up then. Clay Aguirre surprised himself by how scared he was of losing Mira. Last year, when he was a junior, he really loved Naomi Martinez. He took her for granted, he was rude to her, and in the end when it looked like he might be losing her, he hit her. Ever since, there had been a sadness deep in his heart that he would not admit to anyone, even to himself. He was sorry he lost Naomi Martinez. He had a terrible, nagging fear that he would never again find someone who cared that much for him.

Mira Nuñez was not Naomi Martinez, and she never would be. But Clay thought she was the closest thing to Naomi that he would ever meet. She did love Clay, and he loved her. He was not going to blow this relationship like he did the one with Naomi. If that meant looking away when a chick in tight pants appeared, he would abide by that for Mira's sake. Because he did not want to lose her.

Carlotta was speechless. Her mouth was so dry she didn't think she could swallow. She didn't see this coming. She couldn't believe it had happened. Sure, she knew Clay dated Mira Nuñez. Naomi told her. Ernesto Sandoval mentioned it. But Carlotta had not let that deter her before when it came to cute boys. She had broken up several pairs up in Huntington Beach. She had always felt that if the relationship was any good, she couldn't have lured the guy away.

Carlotta threw herself, sobbing, on the bed. Her cries were so loud that Aunt Linda and Uncle Felix came. But their reactions were much different.

"Lotta, honey, what's the matter?" Aunt Linda asked in a soothing voice. She sat down on Carlotta's bed and gently stroked her heaving back.

"Stop your caterwauling, girl," Uncle Felix said. "You're scaring the dog. Poor Brutus is under the kitchen table with his paws over his ears. You wanna give the dog a nervous breakdown? The cats out on the fence are joining in the howling. You wanna upset the whole *barrio*? What's the matter with you? You nuts?"

"Carlotta," Aunt Linda said, "it can't be all that bad. Now tell me what's wrong, dear." She continued stroking Carlotta's back. But Carlotta only sobbed louder.

"I've had it," Felix said. "I'm callin' the cops and tellin' 'em we got a psycho here."

Carlotta Valencia stopped crying. She sat up and dried her face. "It's just that … Clay Aguirre … I thought he liked me … he just called and said he doesn't want to see me anymore."

"Oh, for Pete's sake!" Felix Martinez stormed, going back to the living room.

Tish and Loni were telling everyone at school on Monday that Carlotta Valencia was a shameless flirt, and that she had tried to get Clay Aguirre away from Mira Nuñez but it didn't work. When Naomi heard it, she shook her head and said, "I *told* Lotta to leave Clay alone."

When Carlotta, Clay, Naomi, and Ernesto went to Mr. Davila's class, Carlotta sat as far from Clay as she could. Occasionally she cast Clay a dark look. She was sitting in the back row, and she began texting all her friends in Orange County, telling them how a boy had feigned interest in her and then cruelly cut her off. She was sending her fifteenth text, and the class was only half over when Mr. Davila suddenly stopped talking about American relations with Saudi Arabia. He looked at Carlotta and said, "Carlotta Valencia, I want you to bring your phone to my desk and leave it there until the bell."

Carlotta was shocked. She had thought the teacher had no idea what was going on in his classroom. "What?" she gasped.

"You heard me. Put your phone on my desk," Mr. Davila said. "I'm not going to ask you again."

"*It's my phone,*" Carlotta almost screamed. "You can't just take it!"

"You may pick it up at the end of class," Mr. Davila said. "You have been doing nothing but texting in my class, and it is disrespectful and intolerable! By this behavior, you are saying to me that I am saying nothing of importance. I am very close to asking you to leave this class permanently, but I will give you another chance. If you ever again remove the phone from your purse or tote bag—or whatever you keep it in—during class, you are out of here. I will not be treated with such contempt!"

Tears filled Carlotta's eyes, but she said nothing.

When class ended, Carlotta reclaimed her phone and went rushing from the classroom. Mira Nuñez said in a voice loud enough for everyone, including Carlotta, to hear, "What an idiot! To be sitting there in front of the teacher texting nonstop—a six-year-old wouldn't be that stupid!"

Carlotta turned and said to Mira, "Drop dead!"

"Back to you," Mira said, sneering. Clay grabbed Mira's arm and said quickly, "Come on, babe. Don't bother with her." Clay and Mira hurried off, arm in arm.

"Wow," Naomi whispered to Ernesto, "how awful!"

Carlotta turned to Naomi and Ernesto and tearfully said, "Ernie, you said seniors sometimes tutor kids having trouble in class. Would you please help me? I don't even know what this class is about! I'm totally lost!"

CHAPTER SIX

Ernesto Sandoval looked at Naomi with a bewildered shrug.

"I guess you'll have to," Naomi said. "I'm sorry."

"It's not your fault," Ernesto said. He walked over to Carlotta. "There's a little room in the library. It's got computers and study space. The senior tutor program has it reserved after school for an hour. You can meet me there after your last class, and we'll go at it," he said.

"Oh, thank you, Ernie," Carlotta said. "Because this guy Davila is making no sense to me. He might as well be teaching in Greek!"

"It must be hard to try to listen to the

teacher's lecture and text your friends at the same time, Lotta," Naomi said. "I mean, that's multitasking, big-time."

"Another snide remark, Naomi," Carlotta said. "I'm not surprised. I know you never liked me."

Naomi shrugged and headed for her next class. There was no point in trying to convince Carlotta that Naomi really did like her because she didn't. Wherever Carlotta went, she stirred up trouble. Last year, she almost caused her parents to get a divorce. Her father was so sick of the girl's shenanigans that he was determined to send her to boarding school just to afford the family some peace, but her mother refused to do that. They argued for weeks. Sending Carlotta to the Martinez house was the compromise that saved the Valencia marriage.

After school, Ernesto went reluctantly to the study room in the library to wait for Carlotta. He had promised the senior class that any senior in need of tutoring had only to ask for help. They could count on Ernesto or some other senior. In an eloquent address to the senior class, Ernesto said he wasn't satisfied that just he and his friends would graduate in June. He wanted to bring along each and every senior if he could. He said he refused to leave anyone behind. And, sadly, that now included Carlotta Valencia.

Carlotta came hurrying into the room about five minutes late. "That beast Samson kept us over raving about Ernest Hemingway and how wonderful he was," Carlotta said, rolling her eyes.

Ernesto sighed deeply. "Well, where to begin?"

He turned and looked at Carlotta. "What don't you understand about America as a world power?"

"Well, I know the United States is a powerful country with a lot of soldiers and stuff, and we got nuclear bombs, but Davila keeps talking about our friends and allies and enemies, and I'm getting all mixed up. Like right now, we're talking about

Saudi Arabia. I mean, he says they're our friends but how come they bombed us on nine-eleven?"

"No, no," Ernesto said. "We've always had cordial relations with Saudi Arabia. We have a long relationship with the royal family in that country. Right now, they're helping us by giving us important intelligence about possible terrorist plots."

"But what country did attack us on nine-eleven?" Carlotta asked.

"No country attacked us, Carlotta," Ernesto said. "Little groups of very evil men—terrorists—they attacked us. They have little cells all over the world, including in our own country. They're in Afghanistan, Pakistan, Saudi Arabia, the Philippines, Indonesia. These guys have no power except the power to create violence and death. They're like criminals. No country wants them around, but sometimes a government is too weak to drive them out or arrest them. So the terrorists hide out in the mountains and train soldiers to carry out things like suicide bombings. Sometimes they hang out in an apartment right in an American neighborhood. A couple of the guys involved in nine-eleven lived in a nice neighborhood about ten miles from here."

"Oh, Ernie," Carlotta said, "how did you get so smart?"

"Look, I'm an average guy, Carlotta. I listen to the lecture in class as if my future depends on it, which it does. I take notes. I read the assigned stuff. I go on the Internet and learn as much as I can. It's not rocket science, Carlotta." He turned to the computer. "Let's Google Saudi Arabia."

When information about the country appeared on both their screens, Ernesto said, "See, there's the king. The royal family has been so close to the United States for decades that he comes over here for medical treatment. He dresses in clothing we consider unusual, but he's a smart guy. Mr. Davila wants us to study what Saudi Arabia is doing now to combat terrorism. He wants us to understand how that country is dealing with their own young people who want some changes. Look, Carlotta, there's news right now about a terror plot they tipped us off about … some guy trying to plant bombs in an urban center."

"Wow," Carlotta said. "I've never even looked at this stuff. I'm on Facebook and I read Twitter a lot, but—"

"King Abdullah, he met with Pope Benedict to talk about cooperation among the religions of the world. That's important because people hating one another because of different religions cause a lot of trouble. It's all here, Carlotta. You've got a computer in your room at the Martinez house. Just go and get the information. I know it's a lot more fun to check out iTunes and download your favorite music. I'd rather go home and download the music of the rap group I've started to follow, but I spend most of my time studying."

"But it's so boring," Carlotta said.

"Too bad. You've got to quit texting

in class, listen, take notes, and use the computer to expand what we learn in class," Ernesto said.

They spent a full hour going over the various alliances the United States had in the world and the countries most likely to cause serious trouble in the near future. Carlotta said, "I've learned more from you in the past hour than I learned all year in my history class at my old school. You're a good teacher, Ernie. Are you gonna teach when you finish college?"

"I planned to for a while. My dad is a great history teacher here at Chavez. I wanted to be just like him. But then I decided I'd go to law school like my Uncle Arturo," Ernesto said.

"Boy, you got a great family, Ernie," Carlotta said. "I wish I had a nice family like yours. I bet your parents are never mean and unreasonable."

"Listen, if I screw up, or my sisters do, we get flattened fast. In middle school, I cut a few classes so I could hang with my friends and go skateboarding in this cool new park in LA, and my father came and got me and marched me home, and I was grounded for a month! No TV, no computer games, nothing. I lost all my privileges. That's what being a good parent means, Carlotta. Your parents must love you very much to send you down here so you can learn from Linda and Felix Martinez," Ernesto said.

"I hate it so much in that house, Ernie. I hate Uncle Felix more than anybody. He's like an ogre. He loves to humiliate me. He's so cruel. He's a sadist," Carlotta said.

"Come on, Carlotta. You're way over-the-top here. I've had my problems with Mr. Martinez, but he's no ogre. Underneath that rough exterior, there's a good guy. He wants you to become a better person. He's a good man who loves his family. I have no doubt he'd lay down his life for his wife or any of their kids. Don't lock horns with him, Carlotta," Ernesto cautioned.

Carlotta took a long look at Ernesto. He had thick, dark curly hair; his large dark eyes, full of emotion; his caramel skin that gave him a permanent tan—the kind that most sunbathers would die for. Carlotta envied Naomi that she had such a wonderful boyfriend: handsome, kind, smart. Carlotta did not think Naomi deserved Ernesto.

In a deep, secret part of her heart, Carlotta wondered if she had any chance in the world of winning Ernesto away from Naomi. As she looked at the boy's wonderful, expressive face and saw the compassion in his eyes, she wondered if there was anything she could do to make him belong to her.

Carlotta had never met anyone like him in her life. The thought that he was going to be tutoring her and that she'd have many opportunities to be with him excited her. Maybe lightning would strike. Surely stranger things had happened. Carlotta loved to read about the fabulous lives of movie and TV idols, and she learned that sometimes two actors, both apparently happily married or in a relationship, suddenly looked into one another's eyes, and that was it. Maybe, Carlotta thought, it could happen like that for her and Ernesto.

"Thanks so much for helping me, Ernie," she said. "It was really good."

"We can do it again if you need more help," Ernesto said.

"Thanks," Carlotta said.

"How are you getting home, Carlotta? Naomi already left, and you rode in with her, right?" Ernesto asked.

"Oh, I'll just walk home," Carlotta said. "It isn't far."

"I live on Wren Street, right next to Bluebird," Ernesto said. "I'll drop you off. Here's another chance to ride in an ancient Volvo that is the laughingstock of the school."

"You've done so much already, I hate to—" Carlotta started to say.

"No problem," Ernesto said.

Carlotta felt strange. Was Ernesto feeling some attraction for her, or was he just being nice? Carlotta trembled with excitement at the prospect that this might be the beginning of the most wonderful episode in her life.

That evening, Naomi was sitting out in the little garden filled with the elves her father had carved. A hummingbird was hovering over the spray of water from the small waterfall. The back door opened, and Felix Martinez came out and sat on the stone bench opposite Naomi.

"Naomi, in a couple weeks we're gonna be taking your mother out to dinner at this fancy place for her birthday, you know. You know she ain't never eaten in a fancy place like that with a view of the ocean and all. It's gonna be really special," Felix Martinez said.

"That's great, Dad. Mom will love it," Naomi said.

"Naomi, listen, I usually get your mom a birthday gift that's useful, you know. Something to help her around the house. She's always said she liked that kind of stuff. But … when you took her shopping and got her those stylish clothes, I mean she kinda lit up. She was looking frumpy, and all of a sudden she looked … good. Naomi, I've loved your mother ever since I was a kid, and the way she looks doesn't matter. She's my Linda, and she always will be. When we both get old and funny-looking, she's still gonna be my Linda, and I probably won't even notice the changes, but I forget sometimes that she's a lady, that there's a girl inside there wanting to be pretty," Mr. Martinez said.

Naomi looked at her father, touched by what he was saying. He was such a rough man most of the time that it was easy to forget the softness just beneath the surface, the tenderness that ran deep.

"So, honey, like I said, I've been thinking, you know, you got her pretty stuff, and she liked it. She looked like a movie star or something. And so I thought this time I wouldn't go for the practical stuff. Your mother, she doesn't have any good jewelry.

She's always buying cheap stuff at the drug store. Rinky-dink little necklaces and such. So I went down to the jewelry store the other day on my way home from work. Osterman's, that's a good place. I hadn't been in there before since we got married, and I got the engagement ring and the wedding band. That was the last time I went in there. I saw this necklace and earrings that matched … and she's got her ears pierced you know, and she sticks in those cheap earrings from the drug store, but this stuff was beautiful, Naomi." His voice grew heavy.

"Oh, Daddy," Naomi said, caught between a smile and tears, "that would be so wonderful if you got her something really nice like that."

Felix Martinez smiled a little. "The necklace, it has a diamond, you know, and an eighteen-karat white gold for the chain. And the earrings too. Costs a lot. Over a thousand dollars. The lady there, she said the necklace and the earrings come in a little red box, real elegant. I went back there several times 'cause that's a lot of money, but on Friday, when I came home from work … *I got them.*"

Naomi threw her arms around her father and kissed him. Then she drew back and said, "Daddy, I've always loved you, but never more than I do right now."

Felix Martinez grinned. "Love you more, baby—you and the boys and your mom. So I did the right thing?" he asked.

"Oh, did you ever!" Naomi cried.

"She's gonna be surprised, huh?" Felix Martinez asked, still grinning like a little boy who had pulled off something amazing. "She's gonna see this little box and wonder what kinda kitchen dealy is that? Maybe a one-egg poacher or something." He laughed heartily.

When Naomi and her father went inside, Linda Martinez was making another special dinner, hoping to impress Carlotta. Naomi and the boys—when they were here—were satisfied with any good, hearty meal, but Mrs. Martinez was trying so hard to make her niece happy. Tonight, she was making flounder Florentine, chopped flounder fillets with spinach and red bell peppers.

Naomi and her father went into the living room, and Naomi noticed a strange look in his eyes. He seemed to have moisture there, as if he could cry at the drop of a hat. "Naomi," he said softly, "you know when I got this idea for the jewelry? Remember a coupla weeks ago when your mother went for the mammogram, and they called her back 'cause something didn't look right?"

"Yes," Naomi said.

"Little girl, it hit me then like a ton of bricks how precious she is to me," Felix Martinez said. "I couldn't make it without her, you know?"

When Ernesto dropped off Carlotta, he came in the house and said hello to the Martinezes, and then he kissed Naomi. That disappointed Carlotta, but she still was hoping for a miracle down the line.

Just before dinner, Linda Martinez said,

"You'll like this, Carlotta. I even got some tips from Ernie's friend, Abel Ruiz. He makes the best flounder."

Mr. Martinez said, "Hey, Linda, how come you're bothering yourself? You know what it says in the Bible, pearls cast before the swine ain't such a good idea."

Carlotta cast her uncle a hateful look, but she didn't say anything. Both Ernesto and Clay had told her to try to make friends with the ogre. She didn't think she could, but she decided to at least avoid confronting him.

"You know, Naomi," Mr. Martinez said, "when you and Ernie are together, you won't have any trouble feeding him. All the poor kid wants are peanut butter and jelly sandwiches. Be a snap for you."

Naomi giggled. "Poor Ernie. He's so happy when Abel brings tortilla wraps, and he gets to have something better."

"This flounder is so good," Mrs. Martinez said. "I used spinach and basil and pepper sauce."

"I hate spinach," Carlotta said.

"Hey, listen," Felix Martinez said. "Brutus out there, he ain't eaten all his doggie treats yet. Why don't you go out there and eat with him, Lotta? Then you won't have to eat the spinach and the fish."

"Felix," Linda Martinez groaned.

They all sat at the table while Naomi's mother put out the delicious-looking entrée. The servings of flaky fish were arranged around the spinach.

"Oh, this is wonderful, Mom," Naomi said, tasting it.

"Yeah, it's okay," Felix Martinez said, "but I'd be just as happy with your enchiladas with lots of salsa, Linda."

"Anything would be better than this," Carlotta said, wrinkling her nose.

"You say another word that rubs me the wrong way, Princess Pickle-Face, and you're gonna have flounder and spinach on top of your head with the sauce runnin' into your ears," Felix Martinez said.

Carlotta ate the rest of her dinner in

sullen silence. She had resolved to please Felix Martinez, but she just couldn't get by her hatred of him. She was glad when dinner was over so she could escape to her room.

Carlotta thought about Ernesto again and thought maybe he wasn't as crazy about a girl as slim as Naomi. Carlotta had more curves and a lot of boys appreciated that. That was what drew Clay's attention to her. Carlotta thought if she could just reach Ernesto on a very basic level— maybe excite him by wearing really hot clothing—she might be able to undermine his relationship with Naomi.

Ernesto had told Carlotta to spend some time at the computer studying the Middle East countries they were talking about. She checked out Afghanistan and learned about its history. She thought Ernesto would really be pleased if she made some intelligent comments in class after he spent all that time tutoring her.

Carlotta spent a whole hour Googling Afghanistan and taking notes. Ernesto would be so happy he had made such a good impression on her. That just might be the foot in the door for their relationship. Naomi was very smart, and she was always participating in class, and Ernesto seemed to respect that.

Carlotta was an intelligent girl, and the only reason she didn't make excellent grades was that she was bored by school and studying. She did have a high IQ, and when her parents went to parents' night at that private school, they were always told their daughter was an "underachiever," not working to her potential.

In class, Carlotta would prove to Ernesto that she was as smart as Naomi by making insightful comments. Ernesto would sit up and take notice. And it wouldn't hurt that she would be wearing her tightest jeans either.

Carlotta went to sleep with a smile on her face.

CHAPTER SEVEN

Mr. Jesse Davila opened his class with a question: "Can anybody name some reasons why America's relationship with Afghanistan has been so difficult?"

Carlotta's hand shot up.

Mr. Davila looked surprised, but he said in a pleasant voice, "Yes, Carlotta."

"Well, Afghanistan is located in a very bad place," she said. "Long before the present-day problems came up, this was the invasion route for many foreign empires. The people there have known war since ancient times. In the sixth century, they were invaded by Darius of Persia and then Alexander the Great, and the Turks and the Mongols. After all that tragic violent history, it's hard for the tribes to come together in a unified country."

"Yes," Mr. Davila said, "that was a very good analysis of the country's historic challenges."

Carlotta glanced over at Ernesto, who was smiling broadly.

For the next two weeks, Ernesto spent an hour two afternoons a week tutoring Carlotta. For the first time in her life, Carlotta was doing well in her classes and turning in her homework on time.

Carlotta texted Katy, "I think Ernie has the hots for me! He is so excited and happy for me when I do well." Carlotta could think of no other reason why Ernesto would be spending so much time helping her.

When Ernesto and Naomi went down to the ocean on a cool, windy day, they didn't plan to swim. They wanted to see the big waves crashing on the coastline.

"Carlotta has really changed since you started working with her, Ernie," Naomi said. "She's actually doing schoolwork at night instead of texting and downloading music all the time. She got a B-minus on a math test. She told Mom that was her best math grade since fourth grade."

"That's good," Ernesto said. "She's smart. She's just been too lazy to study before. No matter how smart you are, you gotta study."

"Here comes a big one," Naomi cried, watching the powerful wave curl and then come crashing on the sea wall.

"I never wanted to surf, but I love to watch the waves," Ernesto said.

"Me neither," Naomi said. Then she got a serious look on her face. "Ernie, my dad just blew me away the other day. He's such a tough dude that what he said caught me completely by surprise. Remember when I told you about Mom having to go back and check something after her mammogram? It turned out okay, but Dad was shaken. He told me that it made him think how precious Mom was to him, and he decided that this year he wouldn't get her an appliance for her birthday. He wanted to get her something special."

"That's sweet," Ernesto said. "Good for him."

"Yeah, and he paid a lot of money for a gold chain with diamonds and earrings to match. He's so excited about giving it to her. He said it comes in a tiny red box, and Mom will wonder what kitchen gadget is so small," Naomi said.

"Hey, that's great. That's really great," Ernesto said. "I haven't always gotten along with your dad, Naomi, but I always respected him. Now I respect him more than ever."

"We're going to a real expensive restaurant overlooking the ocean to celebrate Mom's birthday, and he's giving it to her then," Naomi said. "My brothers are coming down to join us, and it's going to be so cool. The problem is what to do about Carlotta. I mean, do we all just leave while she's stuck at home? Or do we let her come too and ruin the whole occasion?"

"Yeah, that is a problem," Ernesto said. "I guess you'll have to invite her. She lives there, and she *is* family. It would really be awkward to exclude her, even though I sure know where you're coming from."

"Yeah, you're right, Ernie. We're stuck. I need you to keep me on track. You've got so much to do, Ernie, your job, track practice, the senior class government, your own classes, and still you spend time tutoring Carlotta. You've really got a big heart," Naomi said.

"Or a soft head," Ernesto sighed. "I usually get along with people, but this girl is a challenge. She's whining all the time, like she's got the worst life of anybody. I'm looking around for somebody else to take over tutoring her 'cause I'm getting weary. A bunch of seniors signed up for the program, and I'm checking for someone who's got time."

Naomi laughed. "I'm embarrassed that she's my cousin. When she says something mean or stupid, other kids will go 'oh, your cousin did such and such,' or 'Naomi, Naomi, guess what *your* cousin did?'"

"Well, at least she'll be going home in a few months, and then it'll be over. And maybe we did her some good. Maybe something that happened here will get through that selfish shell she's built around herself," Ernesto said.

When Mia Valencia called her daughter at the end of the week she said, "Sweetheart, we've been getting all those exciting text messages about your good grades. Your father and I are so delighted. It's a miracle."

"I've been working so hard, Mom. I just work, work, work all the time. I don't get to do anything fun anymore. I'm slaving in this house doing all the cleaning and taking care of this vicious dog, the pit bull. Then I study like crazy. I have such a miserable life, but at least I *have* brought up my grades."

Carlotta didn't tell her mother the main reason she was working so hard on her classes. She wanted to please Ernesto. He had spent so much time helping her that she knew how happy it made him when she did well. Ernesto smiled at her in such a cute way. Carlotta could tell that he was caring more about her every day, and pretty soon he would dump Naomi and become Carlotta's boyfriend. Carlotta was pretty sure of that. All the signs were there.

When Ernesto did dump Naomi for Carlotta, she knew Naomi would be bitter and furious. She would try to make Carlotta's life even more miserable in the Martinez house, but Carlotta didn't care. Anything she had to suffer was worth it if she was Ernesto Sandoval's girlfriend.

"Carlotta, dear," her mother said, "we weren't going to say anything about this until later, but if you graduate from Cesar Chavez High with a good GPA, we will be giving you a very nice graduation gift."

"What is it, Mom?" Carlotta cried. "You've got to tell me."

"We were planning it as a surprise," Mia Valencia said.

"Tell me, oh, please, oh, please," Carlotta screamed.

"You know that Audi you were looking at?" Carlotta's mother said.

"Oh, Mom, oh no! Do you mean … oh, Mom, I'm gonna faint! I'm gonna fall right down now and faint!" Carlotta screamed again.

"You graduate with a B or better, and the Audi will be your graduation present, darling," Mrs. Valencia said.

"Oh! Oh! Mom, I love you! I love Dad! I love both you guys. I'll do it, Mom. I'll study even harder. I'll study like crazy. This boy who's helping me, the one who's falling in love with me, he's gonna help me even more. I can do it! I *know* I can do it. Oh, Mom, you're serious, aren't you? I mean you're not just kidding, are you? I think I'd curl up and die if you were just kidding."

Carlotta was making so much noise that Linda Martinez came to her bedroom door to make sure she was all right. Carlotta was rolling around on the bed, laughing hysterically, the phone on her ear. "Oh, Aunt Linda," she gasped. "I'm on the phone with Mom. When I graduate from Chavez, my parents are giving me a brand new Audi for a graduation present!"

Carlotta handed the phone to Linda Martinez so she could talk to her sister. "Mia, Carlotta just told me she was getting a new Audi when she graduated—" Mrs. Martinez said.

"If she gets a B or more, yes, Linda," Mia Valencia said.

"Do you think that's wise?" Mrs. Martinez stammered.

"Linda, this girl has been a C-minus student. If she can bring her grades up to a B-average, then it's worth it. Linda, I'm sure you've bribed your kids with stuff. We all do it," Carlotta's mother said.

Linda Martinez looked bewildered. "I used to promise the boys I'd make that nutty fudge they liked if they passed their math test," she said.

Carlotta raced to the living room where Felix Martinez was watching TV. "Uncle Felix, my parents are going to get me a new Audi for a graduation present! My mom just told me."

Naomi had just come into the room, and she looked shocked. "An Audi?" she gasped.

"Yes, yes, yes!" Carlotta screamed, dancing around the living room. "If I get all Bs, it's mine! And I can do that. I *will* do that!"

"That's the stupidest thing I ever heard," Felix Martinez growled. "That's the most disgusting thing I ever heard of. You should be making good grades for your own future so you're not a stinking parasite on society. It shouldn't be because you're getting an expensive new car.

"My little girl has an A-average, and she works long hours at the yogurt shop so she could afford to buy her beater. I'm proud of Naomi. She worked for what she got. When stuff is handed to you, it don't mean anything. You don't deserve a new car. Your parents must be crazy."

"You just begrudge me nice things because you're too poor to get good stuff for your daughter," Carlotta accused Mr. Martinez.

"Stop it!" Naomi said sharply. "If my parents had offered to buy me a car, I would have refused it. It wouldn't have really been mine, then. I wanted to save money and get my own car so I could have pride in what I'd done. What Dad says is true. What you get for nothing never makes you happy. I know my car is old, but it's mine, all mine."

Carlotta glared at Naomi. "Just wait," she thought, "pretty soon you'll be getting the nasty shock of your life, girl. Your boyfriend is gonna dump you for me!"

Over the next week, Carlotta continued to make good grades. She ate lunch with Naomi and Ernesto and their friends every day. Carlotta wanted to grab every chance she got to be close to Ernesto. She watched him constantly, looking for little clues that he was admiring her. Every time he smiled, she thought the smile was for her.

Carlotta had noticed that Naomi wore blue a lot, so she thought Ernesto must like blue. Carlotta bought a very pretty lacy blue top. When she wore it for the first time, she asked Ernesto, "Does this top go good with my jeans?"

"Huh?" Ernesto said. He was eating a tortilla wrap Abel had brought for him. Abel took pity on Ernesto when he saw him eating peanut butter and jelly sandwiches three days in a row. This tortilla wrap was stuffed with sliced savory turkey breast, lettuce, shredded cheese, and sliced olives. Ernesto really liked it, and he was focusing on every bite. "Uh, yeah, sure, Carlotta," he finally said.

Carlotta attributed Ernesto's disinterest in her new top to the fact that fish-eyed Naomi was sitting right there next to him, and she'd probably tear his hair out if he showed any interest in another girl's top.

"It sorta looks like something you'd wear to bed," Julio said, focusing on Carlotta's top.

Mona Lisa, Julio's girlfriend, giggled.

Carlotta thought Julio Avila was a mean punk, and she hated him. She hated Mona Lisa too.

"Man, this tortilla wrap is so good, Abel," Ernesto said. "I owe you."

Abel laughed. "It's my pleasure, dude. I owe you for more than that."

"I feel really good about the English test today," Carlotta said. She'd bought an egg salad sandwich from the machines and a slice of cheesecake for dessert. She had added a pound this week. It didn't worry her. She thought it made her look even better in her tight jeans. "I studied all last night for the test."

"Good," Ernesto said, washing down his tortilla wrap with orange juice.

"Ernie, you've helped me so much," Carlotta said in an emotional voice. "I can't thank you enough."

"*Por nada*," Ernesto said. "I promised to help all the seniors make it to graduation, Carlotta, and you're one of the gang. It's all for one and one for all."

"That is so beautiful," Carlotta said in a whiny kind of voice.

"Anybody got a violin?" Julio asked. Mona Lisa giggled again, and Carlotta was so offended by Julio's attitude that she left early.

When Carlotta was gone, Julio said, "I don't know, but something about that chick makes me want to barf."

Naomi covered her mouth to hide a giggle, but Ernesto laughed openly. Abel snickered. "She's such a phony," he said. "Maybe it's not her fault. Maybe her parents are like that too."

As the time for Linda Martinez's birthday party drew nearer, Naomi asked her mother if she was going to invite Carlotta. She really wasn't surprised by her mother's answer.

"Of course, Naomi. Why, it would be so hurtful if we excluded her. I couldn't do such a thing," she said.

"Yeah," Naomi said. She hated the thought of Carlotta coming along, but she agreed they couldn't in all decency leave her out. They had no choice.

"I wouldn't dream of leaving the poor child all alone at home while we went to a nice restaurant and enjoyed ourselves," Linda Martinez said. "That would be so cruel."

When Carlotta came in from putting fresh water in Brutus's water dish, Linda Martinez said, "Carlotta, dear, next Friday night, my family is taking me out to dinner for my birthday. My sons are coming down from Los Angeles too. It's going to be very nice. You'll get to meet Orlando, my oldest son. He's doing so well singing with a Latin band. And Manny plays for the band, and my youngest son, Zack, is coming too. I'm sure you'll like your cousins."

Carlotta vaguely remembered meeting

the Martinez boys a few years ago when they all lived at home. They all seemed like brutish roughnecks, younger versions of Felix Martinez. Carlotta remembered hating them.

Mrs. Martinez continued in her cheerful voice, "We'll be going to this beautiful restaurant overlooking the ocean, and the food is just delightful, I'm told. You can see the lights of the boats in the harbor."

Carlotta had other plans. She had known for a while that this particular Friday night had been set aside for some Martinez event, and she wanted no part in it. For one thing, she did not enjoy being with any of them, and the thought of being trapped for several hours with Felix Martinez and his three boorish sons and that twit Naomi was too terrible to contemplate.

Besides, Carlotta thought that this particular Friday night was her golden opportunity to get closer to Ernesto Sandoval than she had ever been before. This was going to be *their* night.

"Aunt Linda," Carlotta said carefully, "it's real nice of you to want me at your birthday party, but I don't think I can make it. See, I got this huge project in history coming up, and I planned on working all through the weekend."

Linda Martinez actually looked sad. "Oh, Carlotta, can't you do your project on Saturday?" she asked.

"No, Aunt Linda, see, there's not enough time. This project means so much to me. If I can do well, then I'll get an A in Davila's class, and that will be so awesome," Carlotta said.

"But, dear, I feel so terrible leaving you all alone in the house while we're all out having this wonderful time," Mrs. Martinez groaned.

"I wouldn't enjoy the dinner, Aunt Linda, because I'd be thinking about my project all the time. You understand?" Carlotta lied then, "And there's another thing too, Aunt Linda. I know how special this dinner is for you guys, and I'd just

130

feel funny being there. I know Uncle Felix doesn't like me, and I don't even know your sons and stuff. I just think everybody would enjoy themselves more if it was just you and Uncle Felix and your kids. I think that would really be best."

Naomi had been listening, and now she stared at her cousin. Naomi was overjoyed that Carlotta didn't want to come to the dinner, but it didn't make sense that she'd care if she ruined it for everybody. Carlotta wasn't the kind of person who would want to miss out on a great meal at an elegant restaurant because she wanted the Martinez family to be spared her company. That just wasn't her.

And the project in Mr. Davila's class was not due for another *three weeks!*

After Carlotta went to her room, Naomi's mother came to Naomi with a worried look. "Oh, Naomi, I feel so bad. I am very much afraid we have made it clear to poor Carlotta that she's an interloper. I don't think she feels welcome, and that's why she's not coming with us on Friday. That hurts me so much. She's my sister's child, and I wouldn't hurt her feelings for the world. Naomi, would you do me a big favor?"

"Sure, Mom," Naomi said, dreading that she wouldn't like what the favor was.

"Go in Carlotta's room and try to convince her to come with us. It would mean so much to me. Would you do that, Naomi? I know you don't like her, but it really hurts me that she would feel she's not welcome at the dinner," Linda Martinez said.

"Okay, Mom," Naomi said, walking reluctantly down the hall to Carlotta's room. She had been so thrilled that Carlotta wasn't coming, and now she had to try to make her come! That special moment when Dad gives Mom the little red box—Naomi wanted that to be perfect, but Carlotta would find a way to ruin it. She'd probably insult Naomi's brothers. She'd probably drive Naomi's father to anger.

"Carlotta," Naomi said, "Mom thinks you won't come to her birthday party 'cause you don't feel welcome. You *are* welcome, so why don't you come?"

Carlotta turned. "I don't want to spend any more time with you guys than I have to, okay? Tell your mom to go have fun. I'll do just fine," she said.

CHAPTER EIGHT

Ernesto was working on the computer in his room to get the next senior class meeting organized when the phone rang.

"Yeah?" he said.

"Oh, Ernie," Carlotta Valencia sobbed. "Something terrible has happened. The whole Martinez family went off to dinner. I was feeding Brutus just a few minutes ago, and he ran away! He's out there in the dark someplace!"

"*What?*" Ernesto gasped. "Brutus *never* runs away!"

"Ernie, I'm so scared. See, I kicked him by mistake. I didn't mean to, but while I was putting out his food, I sort of tripped on him and kicked him, and the front door was open, and he just took off. Ernie, I'd like to die! Uncle Felix loves that dog, and if something were to happen to him because of me ... if he got hit by a car or was stolen or something, Uncle Felix would kill me! Please come and help me find him, Ernie."

Ernesto sighed. His father was coming down the hall as Ernesto grabbed his car keys. "I gotta run over to the Martinez house. Brutus got out," he said.

"Aren't they all gone to Linda's birthday dinner?" Luis Sandoval asked.

"Yeah, but they left Carlotta, that cousin, at home, and she just called, hysterical, and said Brutus ran out the door. She's scared they'll blame her if something happens to the dog. I'm sure Brutus is hiding in the backyard or something. He'd never go far. I'm just going over there to call him. He'll come to me. I won't be gone more than fifteen minutes."

Luis Sandoval smiled and shook his head.

Ernesto drove to the next street and

parked in the driveway of the Martinez house. As he was getting out of his Volvo, he began calling, "Here, Brutus. Where are you, boy? It's Ernie, your buddy." Ernesto thought all Brutus needed was to hear his voice and that he would come running, tail wagging like a windmill.

Ernesto went to the door and rang the bell. He heard familiar barking from inside the house. A smile came to his face. Good old Brutus was home already! Problem solved. All Ernesto had to do now was pat Brutus on the head, say "Hi" to Carlotta, and go back home. It would end up taking less than five minutes.

The door swung open, and Ernesto immediately noticed the heavy aroma of scented candles. The Martinez family never used candles, much less scented ones. The living room was infused with an eerie light from the candles.

"Uh, so Brutus got home," Ernesto said, a strange feeling of unease coming over him.

"Yes," Carlotta said. "Right after I

called, he came back. Thanks so much for coming over so quickly, Ernie. You're always there for me. You're an angel. Please come in for a few minutes."

"Uh … I told my dad I'd be right back home, Carlotta, so … " Ernesto said. "Uh, what's with the candles?"

"Please, Ernie, just for a few minutes," Carlotta said. In the dim light, Ernesto could barely make her out, but as his eyes adjusted to the scant light, he noticed she was wearing a satin top and close-fitting velvet slacks. Her top had a plunging neckline, highlighted by pearls. She wore sparkling earrings and more makeup than he had ever seen on a seventeen-year-old girl. She looked older.

"Ernie," Carlotta said in a sultry voice, "just have a little wine with me. I want to thank you for all you've done for me, and we could just share a little wine."

"*What?*" Ernesto said in a totally bewildered voice. Then he heard romantic music in the background.

Carlotta drew closer to Ernesto and

137

said, "I've felt for a long time that there was something going on with us. I think you've felt it too. Ernie, the chemistry between us is just going wild. Can't you feel it? I fell in love with you the minute I saw you, and I think you kinda feel the same way. Forgive me, Ernie, but I just had to be with you tonight so that we—"

"*Are you crazy?*" Ernesto almost yelled, backing up.

Carlotta's eyes filled with desperation. She reached out and put her hands on Ernesto's shoulders and said, "I know you don't want to hurt Naomi. I understand. But what we feel for each other can't be denied. All those hours you put in helping me with my classes. You wouldn't have done that unless you cared, Ernie … how you look at me and smile."

Ernesto reached for Carlotta's hands and dislodged them from his shoulders, not in a rough way, but with firmness.

"You tricked me over here with a lie about the dog. You lit all those stupid candles, and you put on that sappy music. You stand there looking like a cheap Las Vegas showgirl. You listen to me, Carlotta, and listen good. Don't you *ever* pull anything like this again. This was a cheap, lousy stunt, and I don't appreciate it. Go and wash all that goop off your face, and throw that outfit you're wearing in the trash. Snuff out those candles, and go to bed, for crying out loud!" Ernesto felt rage as he turned on his heel and went out the door, slamming it behind him.

"Ernie," Carlotta cried, tears streaming down her face. "Ernie, come back!"

Ernesto turned and opened the door again. The girl's makeup was running so bad from her tears that she looked scary. "I don't have any respect for you right now, Carlotta. I am disgusted and offended. I thought you were better than this."

Carlotta's grief and humiliation was turning to fear. "You'll tell everybody at school what happened tonight, won't you? You'll tell the Martinezes, and they'll hate me more than they do now. All the kids at school will mock me and laugh at me, and Felix Martinez will tell my parents, and I'll never get the Audi for graduation. I might as well be dead!" Carlotta's whole body was heaving with sobs.

"As far as I'm concerned, I came over here to find the dog and he came home, period. That's the end of it. Now go to bed." Ernesto slammed the door again, this time harder. He got in the Volvo and backed out of the driveway in a way he never had. He lost a lot of tread in the escape.

When he got home, Ernesto found his father outside looking up at the moon. "A waxing gibbous moon, Ernie," he said. "I teach history but I love astronomy. Ernie? You look mad."

"Yeah, I hate being bothered in the middle of doing something important. Brutus got home fine," Ernesto said.

"Poor Carlotta," Mr. Sandoval said. "It doesn't take much to upset her."

Ernesto said nothing. He was so angry

he wanted to spit, and it would have given him great satisfaction to tell everybody, from his parents to Naomi and all his friends, what a stupid, rotten trick Carlotta had pulled on him tonight. He would have enjoyed going into all the details, from the smelly candles to the horrible elevator music, to how garish and freaky Carlotta looked, almost like someone in a Halloween costume or a horror movie.

Ernesto imagined how shocked and amazed everyone would have been. Naomi did not like her cousin anyway, and this would confirm the worst suspicions Naomi had of the girl. Naomi's dislike of Carlotta would turn to hatred.

Carlotta would become the laughing-stock of Cesar Chavez High.

But Ernesto couldn't do it. He promised he wouldn't, and that was it. He hated gossip anyway, and he wanted no part of bringing down another human being, even someone as stupid and selfish as Carlotta Valencia.

Ernesto kept going over it all in his own mind. That Carlotta was so insensitive that she would try to steal her cousin's boyfriend right in the cousin's own house. Somewhere along the line, Ernesto thought, Carlotta's parents had forgotten to teach her common decency.

But still, Ernesto thought, maybe Carlotta could develop a conscience. She was turning her academic life around. Maybe she could find integrity buried deep inside her soul. Maybe she could become a better person.

That was why, as angry as Ernesto was, he never for a moment considered telling anybody about this night.

Ernesto checked the list of seniors who had volunteered for the senior-to-senior mentoring program, and he found a girl named Elaine Carreño who had free time at the period Ernesto was tutoring Carlotta.

"Hey, Elaine," Ernesto said, "sorry to bother you this late. It's Ernie Sandoval. I've been tutoring a senior girl—Carlotta

Valencia—but I'm really hammered for time. She needs help in math and history, after school on Tuesdays and Thursdays. Think you could fill in for me?"

"Sure thing, Ernie," Elaine said.

"Thanks a million," Ernesto said, breathing a sigh of relief. He planned to have as little to do with Carlotta Valencia in the future as was possible.

The Martinez family came home at quarter to midnight. The three boys had to return to Los Angeles, but they had given their mother a lovely gift. But nothing compared to what had been in the little red box. Linda Martinez was now wearing her diamond necklace and earrings. She felt like a princess. Never in her wildest imagination did she ever expect a gift like that from her husband.

Linda Martinez always believed her husband loved her in spite of his occasional harshness, but now she finally knew how much. As Felix Martinez put the necklace around her neck, he wept. Linda Martinez would never forget that.

Felix Martinez opened the front door to find Brutus whining. "Hey, what's that funny smell?" Mr. Martinez yelled. "Somebody here having a séance or something? Hey, Carlotta!"

"She must be sleeping," Linda Martinez said. "Don't wake her up."

Naomi walked over to the wastebasket in the kitchen to find the remains of the scented candles.

"What the—" Felix Martinez yelled, "No wonder the poor dog is whining. Open the doors and windows to let that horrible smell out."

Naomi opened the windows and turned on the fans. Just then, Carlotta emerged from her bedroom in her pajamas, her eyes red and swollen from crying. Linda Martinez went over to the girl and hugged her. "What's the matter, sweetie? You had second thoughts about not coming with us tonight, I bet. You felt lonely and left behind, you poor little thing. We brought home a doggy bag with some delicious leftovers. I'll heat them tomorrow."

"Carlotta?" Felix Martinez stormed. "Are you nuts or something? What'd you light all those stinking candles for? Look at poor Brutus. His eyes are watering. This joint smells like an opium den or something!"

"Felix," Linda Martinez said, "she feels bad enough that she missed all the fun."

Naomi looked warily at her cousin. Something happened here tonight, something not so good, but Naomi couldn't figure it out.

"I … just read that scented candles help you relax and stuff," Carlotta said in a limp voice.

"Well, don't do stuff like this no more," Felix Martinez growled. "The house stinks. I hate weird smells. It's like drug dealers live here or something. Next thing you know, the smell will be floating over to the neighbors and the cops will be around."

"I'm sorry," Carlotta whimpered. She sat on the couch, and Naomi sat across from her.

"You okay?" Naomi asked.

"No," Carlotta said. "I tried to create an atmosphere of good feelings and love, and it backfired."

"I don't want to hear no more nonsense," Felix Martinez shouted. "The smell is kinda fading out. I guess we'll be okay. We need to go to bed now." He walked over and cradled Brutus's head between his rough hands and said with uncharacteristic tenderness, "Gonna be fine, boy. We'll all feel better in the morning."

Naomi caught up to Ernesto before classes on Monday morning. He smiled and said, "How was the birthday party?"

"It was great. It was so beautiful between my parents," Naomi said. "I'll never forget it as long as I live."

"That's wonderful," Ernesto said. "Your mom's deserved a night like that for a long time, and I take my hat off to your dad for realizing that."

"Ernie, one thing, though," Naomi said. "It was so weird when we got home. Carlotta had lit all these scented candles. The house smelled awful. Dad blew a fuse."

"No kidding?" Ernesto said. "She say why she did it?"

"She said she wanted to create an atmosphere of good feelings and love," Naomi said.

"Beats me," Ernesto said. "Hey, I'm getting Elaine Carreño to take over tutoring Carlotta. It's getting to be too much. I'm stretched too thin."

"Good," Naomi said. "You've been looking tired."

"Naomi, you know our outreach for the freshman kids? Well, there's a little girl who needs a mentor bad. Hannah Navarro is a sweet little girl with wonderful parents, but she's fighting leukemia. She just finished a round of chemo, and she's feeling down. Lost all her hair. We were thinking if we got somebody to be her mentor before our trip to the Anza-Borrego Desert, it would mean a lot to Hannah," Ernesto said.

Naomi saw Carlotta coming along just then. Naomi had never seen the girl looking so depressed. When Carlotta saw Ernesto and Naomi talking, she suspected the worst. They were sharing what happened on Friday night! Carlotta thought she would run away today and hide in a cave for the rest of her life. But then Naomi called out to her, "Carlotta."

Carlotta was shaking as she approached the pair. She studiously avoided looking at Ernesto. "Yeah?" she asked nervously.

"Carlotta," Naomi said, "you know that senior outreach to at-risk freshmen I told you about? Well, we're taking our kids out to the Anza-Borrego Desert this weekend but we got a new girl, Hannah Navarro. She's recovering from leukemia, and she needs a mentor. She's already friends with the student I mentor, Angel Roma. Hannah will need a mentor just temporarily, and I was thinking, maybe you could fill in. What do you think?"

Carlotta couldn't bear to look at Ernesto. She thought he must think she's the most despicable creature that ever walked the Earth. Carlotta thought she could never look him in the eye again.

"How about it, Carlotta?" Ernesto said in a normal voice.

"Uh … what would I have to do?" Carlotta asked.

"Just listen to Hannah. Go for a little walk. Be a friend. It's easy," Ernesto said.

"We pack nice lunches and spend the day in the Anza-Borrego and take pictures and just enjoy the sights. The wildflowers are out now, and that'll be beautiful," Naomi said.

Carlotta stole a quick glance at Ernesto. She did not see the contempt she expected in his eyes.

"Uh … I don't know," Carlotta said. Carlotta had convinced herself that Ernesto really was falling in love with her, and that he just needed one night alone with her for the relationship to flower. She had been totally wrong. He loved Naomi. Carlotta felt shamed and humiliated.

"Hannah's parents are really upbeat about their daughter's prognosis. They're trying to be cheerful for Hannah's sake, but she needs to talk about her fears too. It's like her illness is the elephant in the room that nobody wants to discuss. What you'd be there for, Carlotta, is just to listen to her," Naomi said. "Just let her talk freely and listen. That would mean the world to her."

Carlotta thought that maybe this would be a way to redeem herself. She felt so bad about what had happened on Friday night. She stuffed the satin top with the plunging neckline into the trash. The tight velvet pants went in there too. She couldn't stand to look at them anymore because they reminded her of what an idiot she had been. Apparently, Carlotta thought, Ernesto had kept his promise and told nobody about what had happened.

Carlotta had some hope again. Maybe she could get past this. "I guess I could do that," she said slowly. "I mean, my grandmother had cancer, and I spent a lot of time with her … she's okay now. Yeah, Naomi, you can put me down for the thing in the Anza-Borrego Desert."

"Great," Naomi said.

Ernesto was skeptical, but he didn't say anything. He kept thinking about Friday night and how awful it was, and he wondered if they were doing that poor little girl more harm than good introducing Carlotta as her mentor. But maybe not.

"It's a lot of fun when we go on these trips, Carlotta," Naomi said. "We take pictures, and if we're lucky we spot some wildlife. Abel Ruiz usually packs some wonderful food, and we all chip in for the expenses."

"I can do that," Carlotta said, already reaching in her purse. When she first walked up, her shoulders were slumping, but now she stood a little taller.

"Okay, Saturday morning we all meet at the school," Naomi said. "One of our friends has this really freaky van that the freshmen just love. It's painted really wild, and just riding in it gets things off to a fun start."

"I'll be there," Carlotta promised.

When Carlotta walked away, Naomi looked at Ernesto. "You have a strange look on your face, Ernie. Do you think we're making a mistake taking Carlotta?" Naomi asked.

Ernesto smiled. "Babe, miracles happen, right? Let's hope this is one of them."

CHAPTER NINE

Deprise Wilson was the senior adviser at Cesar Chavez High School, and she went along for the trip into the Anza-Borrego Desert.

"What a funky van," Ms. Wilson laughed as Ernesto took the wheel.

"Yeah, it belongs to Cruz Lopez, and he and his homies painted it pretty wild. But he knows how to keep the engine humming, and its really dependable," Ernesto said. "Plenty room for ten kids too."

They drove through Borrego Springs and then on S22 to a marker on the north side of the road. Ernesto parked the van, and the ten students and Ms. Wilson headed into the wilderness with their backpacks.

Abel Ruiz had distributed all the food and supplies into the eleven backpacks, and he carried a small ice chest in his own backpack to keep the fillings for the sandwiches fresh.

"Look at the strata of hills," Ms. Wilson said. "The colors are just amazing: green, pink, and salmon."

"Why are they colored like that?" asked Richie Lorzano, the student Ernesto mentored. Richie had lost both parents when his father had shot his mother. His father was now in prison, and Richie lived in a foster home.

"Different minerals in the rocks, right, Abel?" asked Bobby Padilla, who'd been a runaway and was now the student Abel mentored.

"You got it, Bobby," Abel said.

Angel Roma, who lived with her mother and grandparents, including a grandmother with Parkinson's disease who needed a lot of help, was the student Naomi mentored. Angel had befriended Hannah Navarro, and

154

she had alerted Naomi to the girl's need for a mentor. Hannah wore a cap to cover her baldness. She lost her hair in her leukemia treatments.

Carlotta Valencia walked with Hannah, but she seemed really ill at ease in this new role as mentor to a freshman girl. Carlotta wasn't at all sure she'd be any good at this, but she wanted to do okay because she was badly in need of some self-esteem herself since that humiliating fiasco with Ernesto at the Martinez house.

Everybody took pictures of the funky ocotillo and the stubby creosote bushes. Then the five freshmen and their senior buddies settled down for lunch.

Abel had everything organized. He had appointed Naomi and Ernesto to bring the drinks from the van, and now he spread a large blanket on the sand. He had sliced Swiss cheese, corned beef, creamy cole-slaw, all in cold packets. He brought dark rye bread and various condiments.

Everybody was raving about how good

the sandwiches were as each senior and the students they mentored sat down to eat. Carlotta sat beside Hannah.

Hannah looked at Carlotta and said, "You're pretty."

"Uh, thanks," Carlotta said, surprised.

Hannah was a sweet-looking girl with big dark eyes and dimples in her cheeks. Maybe when she had her nice dark curls framing her face, she was pretty too, but she looked plain with her little cap. Carlotta wanted to say the right thing to the child, but she had no idea what the right thing was. Carlotta had spent most of her life thinking about her own problems, and it was a new experience to have to deal with somebody else's problems.

"It must be hard to lose your hair like that," Carlotta finally said, and she immediately knew it was the wrong thing to say. She shouldn't be focusing on Hannah's illness, she thought. She should be talking about happy things, like the jackrabbit that had just run down the canyon.

But Hannah did not seem to be upset by the comment. "Yeah, I hated that. I used to have nice curly hair. It started to fall out in big hunks, and then it was all gone and Mama cried, but when she saw me looking at her, she smiled real quick and acted like it was bad that I saw her cry," Hannah said.

Carlotta searched her mind frantically to find something to say next. She said, "My grandmother went through chemo too."

Hannah's big eyes widened, "She did?" she asked.

"Oh yeah," Carlotta said. "Grandma had this pretty, sorta silvery blonde hair that she really liked, and then it all fell out, and she said she felt so ugly."

"Me too," Hannah said. "I felt ugly too. It was awful."

"My grandma went down to the wig store, and she bought three wigs, a silvery one like her hair used to be and a red one and a black one. The red one looked really bad. Grandma looked like a clown," Carlotta said.

Hannah broke out laughing.

"My mother wanted to make Grandma feel good so she told her the silvery wig looked really good, even better than her real hair, but Grandma got mad and said it did not. Grandma said, 'It looks like the devil.' Grandma is the kind of lady who doesn't let people fool her," Carlotta said.

Hannah giggled, and then she said, "My mom wants to make me feel better so she says my little cap is so cute, but it's not. I hate it."

Hannah's expression turned very serious then, and she said, "When I got sick and the doctor said I had leukemia, Mom tried to keep it from me. Dad too. I was scared 'cause I knew what I had, but Mom was fake-perky—upbeat and too smiley, and that just made it worse. When I asked her stuff, she'd just say I shouldn't worry, that it'd be fine. Mom and Dad thought they had to be cheery or else I'd be scared, but I was scared anyway. I didn't want Mom and Dad to put on an act."

"Yeah," Carlotta said. "Sometimes life just stinks, and you gotta face it." She took a big bite of the delicious sandwich Abel had made, and she looked around to make sure nobody was close enough to hear her. Then she said to Hannah, "My parents kicked me out of the house."

"*What?*" Hannah gasped.

"Yeah, they did," Carlotta said. "I wasn't doing so good in school and I cheated. The principal at my school caught me cheating, and she yelled at me, and I yelled back at her and called her a crazy old crone."

Hannah laughed so hard she had to cover her mouth. "You didn't!" she gasped.

"I did, yeah. Then my parents kicked me out and made me move down here where I live with my cousin and her family. My uncle is strange. He made a garden in the backyard, and he carved these horrible little devils. They're all sitting around on toadstools. It's really scary. He's kind of crazy. And he has this really mean dog—a pit bull, and I gotta feed it. It's so ugly."

Both Carlotta and Hannah took bites of their sandwiches and washed them down with soda. Carlotta said, "I gotta live with these people until I graduate, and if I get good grades, my parents are gonna buy me a brand new car. I'm working real hard to get good grades 'cause I really want that car, Hannah. But I've had a lot of bad luck since I moved down here. I saw this cute guy, but he had a girlfriend. I tried to get him away from her, but he wouldn't go for it. Then I saw this other guy who was even cuter, but he had a girlfriend. I tried so hard to make him like me instead of her, but it blew up in my face."

Hannah's eyes got big again. "You tried to steal guys from their girlfriends?" she asked.

Carlotta shrugged. "Yeah, I did. I'm not a goody two-shoes like some girls. I'm kinda bad sometimes."

"I'm bad sometimes too," Hannah admitted. "I cheated on a test, and I stole money from a girl's purse."

"I've done that," Carlotta said. "I stole some lipstick from a store, and the crazy lady ran after me, but I ran faster."

Hannah laughed again. "I took the money I stole from the girl's purse back. Mom made me."

"Yeah, well, people like us, Hannah, we're not really baddies. I mean, we just sometimes do bad things," Carlotta said.

Hannah finished her sandwich and was silent for a minute, and then she asked, "Did your grandma's hair grow back?"

"Yeah," Carlotta said. "It looked even better than before. It was nice and soft and silky."

"I hope mine grows back too," Hannah said.

There was another long period of silence, and then Hannah said, "Did your grandma get better or—"

"Yeah, she's going strong now," Carlotta said.

"I bet you were happy when she got

well," Hannah said. "I got a grandma, and I'd feel awful if she got really sick, and … you know … didn't get … well."

"Oh, I'm glad she got well and all that," Carlotta said. "But she's kinda mean. She doesn't like me at all. I got two little sisters, and she's crazy about them. When I was younger, Grandma would come around at Christmas to bring my sisters great stuff. She'd bring me a yucky little box, and she'd go, 'If you were sweet like your sisters, I'd bring you something nice too.' "

Carlotta thought for a moment, and then she said, "Actually, nobody in my family likes me very much. I'm not a suck-up. That's why a lot of the kids in school don't like me either. Nobody really likes me, but I don't care."

Hannah didn't say anything.

Abel had brought small apple tarts for dessert. Hannah looked up and said, "Carlotta, *I* like you."

Carlotta was taken by surprise. "Huh?" she said.

"*I* like you," Hannah repeated. "You're fun."

Most of the other seniors and their freshman buddies hiked around and looked at the incredibly blue Salton Sea, but Carlotta and Hannah spent most of the time just talking.

Carlotta swallowed. "I like you too, Hannah," she said. "You're a pretty cool kid. Kinda tough like me."

"I like talking to you. I can tell you stuff I can't tell my parents, like that I'm afraid I won't get better. I can't tell my parents that 'cause Mom'll cry. But when I can't talk about it, then I'm even more scared," Hannah said.

"Yeah," Carlotta said, "that's the worst, not being able to talk about it. But parents are weird. I can't tell my parents *anything*." Carlotta grinned a little then. "I guess it's lucky we ran into each other, huh, Hannah?"

Hannah grinned too and said, "You bet!"

After Ernesto dropped everyone off at their houses, he drove Naomi and Carlotta toward the house on Bluebird Street. "So how did it go with Hannah?" Naomi asked. "She seemed in a good mood when we dropped her home."

"It went good," Carlotta said. "She's a nice kid. I wish my stupid sisters were like her. Hannah has these dumb parents who want to pretend nothing is wrong with her, and she can't even talk to them about being scared of dying and stuff. Her parents are clueless. But me and her hashed it out, and we agreed that life stinks sometimes, but you hang in there."

"That's great, Carlotta. I think you did her a lot of good," Naomi said.

Carlotta had been carefully avoiding meeting Ernesto's gaze since that disastrous night. Every time she came close to looking at him, she flashed back to the anger on his face in the flickering candlelight.

But now Carlotta got the courage to look at Ernesto and she said, "Hannah did me a lot of good too."

Ernesto smiled.

Carlotta went to her room, and Naomi and Ernesto went out to Felix Martinez's little garden to talk. It was a warm evening, and the sound of the little waterfall was refreshing.

"I'm pleasantly surprised that Carlotta and Hannah hit it off so good. I was really worried about that frail little girl and how Carlotta was going to deal with her," Naomi said.

"Yeah," Ernesto said. "I looked at them several times during lunch, and Hannah was giggling. In some weird way, they connected. Go figure." Ernesto reached over and grasped Naomi's hand, which was soft and tender like a satin pillow. "You got good instincts, babe."

They heard a strange clicking sound then, and they both looked up into the tall Washington palm in the front yard. Within seconds, a beautiful white owl swam through the darkness.

"He's got a chick too," Ernesto said with a grin. "And he's hurrying home."

Naomi put both her arms around Ernesto and whispered, "I love you."

At school, Carlotta felt strange eating with Naomi and Ernesto and the gang. So she found a nice quiet spot near the library and ate her chicken salad sandwich alone. Within a few minutes, a shadow fell across her.

"Hey, you're too pretty a chick to be eating solo," Rod Garcia said.

Carlotta had heard about Rod Garcia. He ran for senior class president but Ernesto Sandoval beat him. Since then, Rod disliked Ernesto. Rod and his friends also got in some trouble recently hassling some homeless man on Washington Street. But Rod was running on the track team, and he seemed to have put his troubles behind him.

"I'm Rod Garcia," he said. "Maybe you've seen me running on the track team."

"No," Carlotta said. "I'm new here. I used to go to a private school in Orange

County, and now I'm down here living with my cousin and her family. Naomi Martinez is my cousin."

"Mind if I join you?" Rod asked, sitting on the other end of the bench.

"No, that's okay," Carlotta said. Rod wasn't as hot as Ernesto or Clay, but he was cute. "I'm Carlotta Valencia."

"Hi, Carlotta," Rod said. "Boy, it can't be much fun living with Felix Martinez and his crowd. He's a hothead, and Naomi can be a pill too. She and Ernie kinda swagger around campus like they're king and queen or something."

Carlotta laughed. "I hear you," she said.

"Ever since Ernie got to be senior class president, he's been throwing his weight around," Rod said. "He comes up with these harebrained ideas and pushes them on the whole class. The guy isn't into football or anything, and he's driven down school spirit. Actually, he's on some big ego trip."

"Yeah," Carlotta said. She didn't personally see that in Ernesto, but she didn't want to disagree with a guy who wanted to sit and have lunch with her. So far, Carlotta had been batting zero in the boyfriend department, and she hoped this Rod Garcia might provide a little fun.

The more that Carlotta looked at Rod Garcia, the hotter he began to look.

"You got a boyfriend, Carlotta?" Rod asked.

"Uh, not right now," Carlotta said. "I had some up in Orange County but not down here."

"It must have been hard leaving your school in the middle of the senior year," Rod said. "What went down?"

"Well, I let my grades slip a little, and my parents came down on me like a tsunami. They are so unreasonable. A couple bad grades and they pack me down here to live with my aunt and uncle, who I totally hate," Carlotta said.

"Carlotta, maybe you and I could hang out," Rod said. "On Friday night, we're going to a concert, and it's supposed to be

168

really great. Tweaked-out instrumentals. Hip-hop underground. I been to hear this group before, and members of the band leap into the crowd while everyone is jumping. You can just inhale the energy. I think you'd have fun."

"Yeah," Carlotta said. "I'd like that. She had begun to fear that all the rest of her senior year would be lonely and dismal. Now, suddenly, there was light at the end of the tunnel. This dude could be her ticket to some fun.

Carlotta began to plan to sell Rod Garcia to Uncle Felix. She decided to tell Uncle Felix that Rod was Clay Aguirre's friend, although Clay and Rod had stopped hanging out together. Still, Felix Martinez didn't know that. Carlotta knew how much her uncle liked Clay, and it probably would be easy to sell Rod as Clay's buddy.

CHAPTER TEN

Carlotta waited until Naomi wasn't home to tell her aunt and uncle about the Friday night date with Rod Garcia. "Aunt Linda," Carlotta said, "this really nice senior at Chavez wants me to go to a concert with him on Friday. He's a good friend of Clay Aguirre's."

"Oh, that would be nice," Aunt Linda said.

"Well," Uncle Felix said. "You been bringing up your grades and doing your chores okay, so I guess it'd be okay. You haven't been causing too much trouble around here except for the night you stunk up the house with those scented candles. Naomi told us you did good out on the desert with that little girl who's sick, so I guess you deserve a night out. If the kid is a friend of Clay's, then he's okay with me."

"Okay, I'll call Rod and tell him," Carlotta said cheerfully. "Thanks, you guys."

Rod Garcia did not come into the Martinez house when he picked up Carlotta on Friday night. Ernesto Sandoval was one of the few guys who did that. Carlotta saw Rod pull up in his car, and she turned to Aunt Linda and said, "Oh, he's here."

Aunt Linda gave her niece a hug and said, "Have a good time, sweetie."

Carlotta and Rod drove to a small club where four guys were performing hip-hop. The crowd was mostly college students. One of the rappers was especially electrifying. He could really move to the beat.

"Blaze writes his own songs," Rod said.

"Is he the guy in the red shirt?" Carlotta asked.

"Yeah, he's going places. One of his videos went viral on YouTube," Rod said.

After the concert, Carlotta thought they might stop at a hamburger or taco stand for something to eat, but Rod said, "My brother and his roomies have a cool condo on Oriole. They're all in college. My brother ordered pizza and drinks, so I thought we could finish up there if it's okay with you, Carlotta."

"Sure," Carlotta said. "I love pizza."

Rod had called the condo "cool," but Carlotta thought it looked shabby. The apartment had four units, and they went up some rickety steps to reach the unit. The paint on the stairs railing was peeling, and one of the front windows was broken, but you could already smell the hot pizza that had just been delivered.

"This is my chick, Carlotta," Rod introduced her. "Carlotta, this is my older brother, Dan, and those bad dudes over on the couch are his college buddies. Carlotta got busted at her school up north, and now she's a senior at Chavez."

Dan Garcia was heavier than Rod, and

he was unshaven. Carlotta thought he looked like a brute. He ogled Carlotta and said, "I like your jeans, girl. Fit you real well."

One of the other boys was drinking a can of beer. His eyes looked glazed like he'd already had quite a few cans. "Nice-looking chick, Rod," he said.

Carlotta sat on the lumpy couch as far from the boys as possible. The couch smelled dirty. But Carlotta took a slice of pepperoni pizza and startled nibbling on it. She was glad when Rod sat beside her.

"So you're from up north?" a boy asked Carlotta. "Lots more goin' on up there. This is kinda a dead town, especially in the *barrio*. Too many old dudes."

"Yeah," Carlotta said, "I liked it up in Huntington Beach. I'm going back there after I graduate from Chavez."

Dan Garcia got another case of beer from the refrigerator and said to Carlotta, "Wanna beer?"

Carlotta had drunk beer before but she didn't like it. But she didn't want to appear to be some goody-goody, so she said, "Sure." She drank the ice-cold beer quickly. It tasted better than the one she had tried before.

Rod Garcia was drinking something other than beer. Carlotta asked, "What's that?"

"A margarita. Wanna sip?" Rod said.

"Oh, I've had margaritas before. My parents serve them all the time, but they're really weak." When Carlotta tasted Rod's margarita, it was much stronger. Carlotta felt a little light-headed.

"Drink up, babe," Rod said. He looked strange. He looked like he was getting drunk.

"Yeah, sober chicks aren't any fun," Dan Garcia laughed.

Carlotta had her first small inkling of fear. The moment she stepped into this place, she didn't like it. It got steadily worse. It was dirty and smelly, and the guys gave her the creeps. Now all the guys were drinking steadily, and pretty soon Carlotta feared they'd be acting crazy. "Rod, I think I've had enough pizza," she said.

"Going home?" Rod cried. "Babe, we've only just begun to have fun!" Everybody laughed at that.

She turned to Rod and said, "I promised my aunt and uncle I'd be home early. I don't want to get in trouble with them. Can we please go now, Rod?"

Rod was finishing his margarita. "Babe, it's early. Chill out." He came close to Carlotta and put his arms around her. He tried to kiss her but she wriggled free.

"Hey!" Rod said.

"I want to go home," Carlotta said in a high-pitched voice. She looked over at the door she had come through when she entered this place, but here were two drunken guys in her way, blocking any escape.

"Come on," Rod said, reaching for Carlotta again. "Don't be like that." He tried to pull her down onto the dirty couch. Carlotta stared around desperately. She looked down the hall to the bathroom. She took off running, getting inside the messy little bathroom and locking the door from the inside.

The bathroom smelled terrible. Between eating too much pizza and drinking the beer and the margarita, Carlotta was sick. But she was more terrified than sick. She looked around the bathroom, hoping there was a window she could crawl through, but it had no windows, just a fan in the ceiling that didn't work.

Rod pounded on the door. "Come on out, Carlotta, or I'll bust down the door."

"We're coming in, babe," one of the other boys yelled. To emphasize his point, he started kicking at the cheap door.

Tears streamed down Carlotta face. The guys were drunk. They looked like brutes. They probably *were* brutes. Who knew what they were capable of?

Carlotta grabbed her cell phone. If she called the Martinez house, Uncle Felix would come get her, but he would never forgive her. Her life in that house would become a living nightmare. Everything good she had accomplished, the better grades, working with Hannah, doing her chores, it was all down the drain. Uncle Felix would call Carlotta's parents, and she would have no Audi waiting for her at graduation, no matter what kind of a GPA she had.

Her hands trembling, Carlotta called the only person who would come and help her under these circumstances.

"Hi," Ernesto said, turning down the volume on his computer.

"Ernie, this is Carlotta. I went on a date with Rod Garcia, and he took me to this apartment with three other guys—older guys—and they got drunk and started grabbing at me. I ran into the bathroom, and I'm hiding in here. But they're banging on the door. Oh, Ernie, I'm so scared!"

"Wait a minute," Ernesto said. "Is this another of your stunts? Because if it is—"

"No, Ernie," Carlotta sobbed. "I'm really scared. I'm in an apartment on Oriole—a green apartment. Upstairs on the right, number four. Oh, Ernie, please help me. They're drunk, and they're trying to get in the bathroom."

Ernesto turned to his father. "That nitwit Carlotta, she's in an apartment on Oriole with three older guys, all drunk, and that creep Rod Garcia. She's barricaded in the bathroom, and they're trying to get in."

"Let's go," Luis Sandoval said.

"Carlotta," Ernesto said, "hang on, we're coming."

Ernesto and his father ran to the car. Ernesto's dad drove while Ernesto called Paul Morales. He told him the situation and Paul said, "Me and Cruz and Beto are just chilling here. We'll get there fast as we can."

"Oh man," Ernesto said to his father, "that girl is beyond stupid. She gets into a party with a bunch of drunks!"

Luis Sandoval shook his head.

They reached the apartment on Oriole in three minutes flat. Coming from Cardinal

Street was Cruz's van carrying Paul and Beto. The van parked behind the car, and the four boys and Luis Sandoval charged up the stairs.

Luis Sandoval reached the door first. He heard someone inside the apartment yelling, "We almost got the door open. We're comin', babe!"

Ernesto's father hit the door hard and shouted, "Open up, you guys!"

There was immediate silence. In a few seconds, Rod Garcia appeared. He looked in horror at his history teacher from his junior year. "Mr. Sandoval, what're you … I mean … nothin' going on here," he stammered.

Luis Sandoval, followed by the four boys, hurried into the apartment and went down the hall to the bathroom.

"Carlotta," Ernesto said, "you can unlock the door. It's safe."

Rod Garcia stared at the three boys with Ernesto. They were muscular and burly with tattoos, and two of them had shaved heads. One of them, Paul Morales, had a rattlesnake tattooed on his hand. They looked like gangbangers. They looked like they were capable of anything.

Paul, Cruz, and Beto remained in the front room looking menacingly at the four boys. Paul pulled out a switchblade and began tinkering with it casually. Rod Garcia's eyes enlarged. The three college students shrunk into the side of the room.

Carlotta was shaking so badly that she could barely unlock the door. Finally she did, and she came out slowly. Her eyes were red from crying.

"Are you okay, Carlotta?" Ernesto asked.

"Yeah," Carlotta whimpered. "I was so scared. They were trying to break down the door. Oh, Rod said we were going to a concert, and it'd be good. And we did, but then we came here, and the guys got drunker and stuff. They started grabbing at me. I begged Rod to take me home, but he wouldn't. I ran into the bathroom and locked the door, but I was so scared they'd get in and … oh, thanks for coming. I didn't know where to turn. I've never been so scared in all my life!"

"Carlotta," Luis Sandoval said, "our car is parked down there in the driveway. Go down there and get in and wait for us. We'll be along in a few minutes."

Carlotta nodded meekly and didn't even look at Rod Garcia as she hurried through the front door and went down the shabby stairs to the car. She crawled in the backseat and closed her eyes. She was still shaking.

"Okay, Rod," Luis Sandoval said. "You brought a seventeen-year-old girl to this apartment where you knew there were older guys who were drunk. What were you thinking?"

Rod Garcia had sobered from fear and shock. "It's my brother's apartment. I uh … hang out here all the time. These guys are Dan's friends. They're good guys. There was nothing for Carlotta to be afraid of. We didn't do anything. That chick just freaked.

She's crazy. I mean, *we didn't do anything*. I'll just go home now. My car is parked on the street."

Rod moved toward the door, but Mr. Sandoval moved into his path. "Give me your keys, Rod, or so help me, I'll deck you. You're drunk. No way are you driving away from here in your condition. What's your home phone number?" Ernesto's father asked.

"You can't … call my folks. They'll …" Rod gasped.

Luis Sandoval turned to Paul and Cruz. "Maybe you guys could find the phone number in his wallet. Don't rough him up too bad, though," he said.

Rod gave Mr. Sandoval his home phone number as Paul and Cruz moved closer.

"This is Luis Sandoval, history teacher at Cesar Chavez High," Ernesto's father said. "Am I talking to Rod Garcia's mother? Good. Your son, he's very drunk over at his brother's apartment on Oriole Street. He wanted to drive home, but we stopped him.

He and his brother and their friends had a drunken party going on, and they terrorized a seventeen-year-old girl. Yes, I would suggest you come at once to pick up your son. You'll be hearing from Ms. Sanchez, the principal at Chavez, so be ready to go in with your husband to discuss this outrageous behavior."

They waited for Mrs. Garcia to show up. She arrived in fifteen minutes. She glared at her son and snarled, "You are so busted! How dare you?"

"Mom," Rod said, "we didn't do anything. We just—"

Luis Sandoval turned to Dan Garcia and the other two boys. "I don't know what the young lady will want to do about this, but we're ready to back her up, so you guys better hope and pray she doesn't want to press charges for anything."

"We didn't do anything," Dan Garcia said. He was very pale.

Luis Sandoval and the three boys left the apartment, followed by Ernesto. At the bottom of the stairs, Ernesto thanked his three friends for backing them up before they drove off in Cruz's van.

Carlotta was huddled in the backseat of the car when Ernesto climbed in beside her. His father took the wheel. "I never thought this would happen," Carlotta said in a soft, hurt voice. "Rod seemed so nice. He's a friend of Clay Aguirre's. Uncle Felix said Clay is a good guy."

Ernesto sneered.

"I'm totally destroyed," Carlotta groaned. "I've tried so hard to do better, and now this. Uncle Felix hates me so much already. When he hears about this, he'll never trust me again. How can I face him and Aunt Linda?"

"We're going to our house first, Carlotta," Luis Sandoval said. "So you can settle down. You made a bad choice in accepting a date with Rod, but it wasn't your fault. He's a student at Chavez, and you had no reason to believe that would happen. You didn't do anything wrong. In fact, by calling Ernie, you did something very smart."

Luis, Ernesto, and Maria Sandoval sat drinking hot chocolate and talking with Carlotta in the kitchen of the Sandoval home.

"Carlotta, did they do anything to you that would require the police to be brought in?" Luis Sandoval asked.

"No," Carlotta said. "I just panicked when Rod wouldn't take me home, and they were all so drunk, but I don't want to call the police. I don't think they would have really hurt me but …"

"Okay," Mr. Sandoval said, "we'll take you home and tell your Uncle Felix and Aunt Linda that you went to a party, that you felt sick so you wanted to come home early, and that Ernesto brought you. We don't have to go into any other details."

Carlotta looked up, tears filling her eyes. She wiped them off her face fiercely with the back of her hand. "All my life, when horrible things happened," she said,

"I always thought it was somebody else's fault. My parents and my grandma were mean. The teachers were unfair. They hated me. My friends were snobs and witches. Uncle Felix is an ogre … but … but … it was me all along. *It was me all along.* It was horrible, wretched, stupid me all along."

Maria Sandoval put her arms around the girl. "Sweetheart, it takes some people a lifetime to realize the truth of what you just said, and you're only seventeen," she said.

Carlotta sobbed. "Oh my gosh, I've been such a huge disappointment to everyone. I've been selfish and shallow," she wailed. "There's been so much bad blood. But I'm the cause! *Me*! I made everyone hate me."

"Nobody hates you, honey. You're growing up. It's difficult, and there are hard lessons to learn. But you are learning," Maria said.

"I've been so horrible to you, Ernie. I'm so sorry. I know you love my cousin," Carlotta confessed. "I want to be a better friend. And a better cousin to Naomi. If you'll let me."

"Naomi is the best person I've ever met. She'll welcome you with open arms—we both will. I don't think there'll be any more bad blood," Ernesto said. "Let's start over. Okay? Hello, my name is Ernesto Sandoval."

Carlotta extended her hand to meet Ernie's. "Hi," she said. "I'm Carlotta Valencia, Naomi's cousin. It's nice to meet you too."